Taobao

OTHER TITLES BY DAN K. WOO

Learning How to Love China

BAO BAO

stories

Dan K. Woo

Published by Buckrider Books
an imprint of Wolsak and Wynn Publishers
280 James Street North
Hamilton, ON L8R2L3
www.wolsakandwynn.ca

Editor for Buckrider Books: Paul Vermeersch | Editor: Jen Sookfong Lee |
    Copy editor: Jennifer Hale
Cover and interior design: Michel Vrana
Cover image: "The fish are fat, the lotus is fragrant" by Liu Zhongfu (刘忠福),
    1987, June. Courtesy of Landsberger collection.
Author photograph: Mengsha Studio/Gong Shoupeng
Typeset in Adobe Caslon Pro, Break Loose
Printed by Rapido Books, Montreal, Canada

Printed on certified 100% post-consumer Rolland Enviro Paper.

10 9 8 7 6 5 4 3 2 1

Canada Council
for the Arts
Conseil des Arts
du Canada
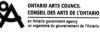
ONTARIO ARTS COUNCIL
CONSEIL DES ARTS DE L'ONTARIO
an Ontario government agency
un organisme du gouvernement de l'Ontario

The publisher gratefully acknowledges the support of the Ontario Arts Council, the Canada Council for the Arts and the Government of Canada.

Library and Archives Canada Cataloguing in Publication

Title: Taobao : stories / Dan K. Woo.
Names: Woo, Dan K., author.
Identifiers: Canadiana 20220159394 | ISBN 9781989496510 (softcover)
Subjects: LCGFT: Short stories.
Classification: LCC PS8645.O472 T36 2022 | DDC C813/.6—dc23

for popo, mom and wife

Contents

Part One: Chastity

1.
The Marriage Market

THE DAUGHTER HAD BEGUN TO LIE TO HER MOTHER, WHO wanted her to get married. "I already have a boyfriend," the daughter said.

It was believable. After all, she was slim, had fine shoulder blades and long, toned limbs. Her face was neither especially like a man's or a woman's. When she put her hair up or hid it under a cap, she felt like a beautiful boy. Her hands were smooth and nice.

Because of her appearance, a few men looked in her direction. Nobody told her what they wanted, but she knew from the way their eyes lingered, as if by looking they could capture a piece of her. She shivered. She had no wish to be possessed by a man.

Her family were Suzhou people. After growing up, the daughter had gone to Shanghai for a year. Her mother had wanted her to come home, to get married, to get caili, a bride price, which would help out her brother, a young baby boy. After three abortions, they'd finally had the son they had been hoping for.

The daughter preferred the glamour of life in Shanghai. For example, she had recently tried something called 'Italian gelato,' a kind of rich, smooth ice cream, which she loved. And although she didn't have enough money to indulge, she liked seeing the large number of beauty spas. "One day I'll treat myself to a relaxing time," she whispered. Besides that, the streets were clean, and she enjoyed window-shopping. Just the multitude of stores and boutiques delighted her. Yes, it was different from other parts of the country she had seen, especially the countryside, where garbage was strewn everywhere around village houses and roads. She couldn't stand the smelly trash and litter.

But, after a while, Shanghai became unpleasant too. The cost of living was too high. She couldn't land any good jobs, and she didn't want to compromise herself. Some men had offered her work in questionable industries, but she didn't accept. She had walked by a storefront with dim red lights one evening, on an unfamiliar street. In the shadows, a neon barber pole turned round and round. A man came out of the door, hiding his face with his hand, while a girl in heavy makeup looked out the glass window. The look on the girl's face had been both bored and unhappy.

Eventually, with her mother bothering her every week to return home, she left. Of all the things she didn't like about Shanghai, it was a new city policy that made up her mind.

"There's a new city ordinance in effect," she said on the phone to her mother. "It's garbage separation. It's so annoying."

"Oh yeah? We don't have it here; I can do what I want with the garbage, throw it all over the road if I want."

"An aunty stands on the road watching us split up the garbage. It's so complicated, and I don't want to get a fine or thrown in jail."

"How does it work?"

"You have to put the garbage in different buckets, according to what it is. They have a jingle to help us remember." The daughter recited the song:

"If the pig can eat it, it's wet garbage.

"If pig can't eat it, it's dry garbage.

"If piggy gets sick and dies, it's poisonous garbage."

"What's that all about?" asked the mother. "Whose pig are you talking about?"

So she went home. Her mother and father were old Suzhouers who once lived in a courtyard house in the old city centre. When the government took back the land, the family was given two sets of apartments in the suburbs. The mother worked sweeping the streets. It wasn't an upper-class job, but at least it was a government job. And because they owned property, they considered themselves rich, upper-class people. The daughter got a job as a shop assistant.

The daughter liked eating, especially watermelon and banana, even drinking cold ice water. When it was available, she would eat crab and mango. When her period came, her mother forbade her from eating these foods, which were depleting for women who were bleeding, but the daughter couldn't help herself. During her period she craved ice cream more than ever. It was such a cold food; the mother didn't understand it. The daughter would sneak out to a shop and buy an ice cream bar or a Popsicle and eat it in the alley.

The mother saw her from the window and scolded her when she went inside. "Whoever heard of this, eating ice cream on your period. You'll get sick."

The daughter wouldn't listen, however.

"I'll make you a wuji soup, or do you want paigu soup?" the mother asked. Everyone liked that kind of soup, and it would boost her warmth, her blood. But the daughter refused.

One morning, the daughter emerged from her bedroom in a baggy sweatshirt and ripped jeans.

"Why do you want to ruin your beauty with such bad fashion?" her mother asked. "You're not a boy, so don't dress like one."

"I like to dress comfortably."

"Your second cousin Little Three just got engaged to a handsome, well-to-do bachelor, the son of a rich businessman. Does she dress like you?" The mother let out a deep breath, her shoulders sagging. "I used to make fun of Aunt Reng's child, that ugly daughter. But even Little Reng is married now. Last year she married a fellow in Peace Town, not too far. He runs a mantou shop." She shook her head. "I'm the one everyone is laughing at now."

As it happened, there was a young man whom the daughter had been ignoring for some months. This was her so-called boyfriend.

The two had met only once, in a little hat shop where the daughter had stopped to try on a visor. He was the shop clerk. He wasn't a very handsome guy, but he wasn't a slob either. If anything, he was decently dressed, taller than her, with carefully trimmed hair and an unblemished face. But he was too eager, which gave away his intentions.

"Hey, there," he had said. "Do you like that hat?"

"Well, kind of."

"You're really pretty, you know?"

She shook her head. It wasn't his straightforwardness she disliked. It was something else she couldn't quite articulate.

"Say, do you want to go on a date with me?"

"You probably say that to all the girls who shop here," she said. She examined a few more hats, not interested in looking him in the eye, or at his face.

"You remind me of Angelababy. She's a terrible actress, but she's pretty. Let me buy you dinner some time."

"No, sorry."

"At least give me your QQ."

"I don't like using QQ," she said.

"Here, then, give me your WeChat." He held out his phone, awkwardly, until she tapped in her contact info.

She received texts on her phone, a growing list of WeChat messages that she didn't answer. They were mostly photos or animated GIFs. One day, feeling bored, she replied to a communication. To her surprise, he instantly replied with a flood of texts.

Is this guy staring at his phone, waiting for my reply all day? He doesn't need to work?

Twice he had ordered food for her, delivered by a Meituan boy. The first was a big plastic cup full of orange bubble tea, crammed with orange ice cream and sealed at the top. She drank it, enjoying the ice cream as usual, but otherwise quite unmoved. The other meal was some deep-fried chicken and potato fries from a new shop that had opened in the city. It came with some wadisu dessert, a crumbly kind of wheat baked in oil. She ate it, but that was all. She guessed he hadn't much experience with love himself and was probably just as confused as any other young man.

Feelings of affection have to be reciprocated in order for a relationship to qualify as a romance, that much the daughter knew. Besides the food, the boy claimed he would send her some gifts in the mail. But she hadn't received anything yet. She thought to herself, *Perhaps once he sends a real gift, I'll like him.*

She was open-minded, or at least, she wanted to be. She wasn't blind to the practicalities of family life, marriage, children, the honour it would bring one in society.

A young Chinese man and a young Chinese woman, together, happy and in love, that's what everybody wants, she thought. *That's what I should want too.*

However, the thought of marrying a man made her feel so nervous and sweaty, she rushed to find the coldest thing to eat, the coldest thing that could slow her quickly beating, liquid-hot heart. And then she felt like herself again.

The mother was a practical person who wanted to solve the problem of her daughter's marriage once and for all.

Neighbours were gossiping, relatives whispered behind their back. The mother came up with a plan. "Why not marry Jujube Lou?" her mother asked. "He's a nice local boy, what more could you want?" Everyone thought Jujube Lou was wealthy because of his prosperous-looking body.

The daughter didn't want that, and the mother could not understand. "Be reasonable. You might like the boy you're dating.

But whatever the case, you want to get the best deal, you should compare them," said her mother. "Maybe Aunt Lou's son can offer us a higher bride price, and a nicer apartment for you to live in."

Soon they were at Aunt Lou's house. It was a spacious apartment, bigger than theirs. As well, they noticed a large bag of expensive jitou rice in the kitchen. Jujube Lou appeared and sat down in the living room, in front of the daughter.

On first impression, she didn't know what to think of him. The boy was several years older than her – a suitable age, it could be said. It was true that he wasn't very tall. He didn't have the kind of look – even features, wide eyes – the daughter liked in a boy, or in a person, for that matter. To make things worse, he had an oily face and his teeth were discoloured. A bad odour came from the boy's mouth, or maybe it was his nostrils.

But all in all, the boy was a traditional, devoted son, perfect in every other way. The bachelor's parents were wealthy and could provide a decent bride price. The mother stood off to one side, hands clasped, rubbing her fingers together.

"I know my daughter's a beauty, but what's the point if she wastes it? Look at her hands, she doesn't know how to do house chores. She's useless to her mother and father and disappoints her younger brother."

"She has such delicate hands," said Aunt Lou.

"Go for a stroll, you two." She nudged the daughter. Aunt Lou clapped her support, encouraging the two young people to go out.

"My son is the nicest gentleman. He deserves a pretty wife. He didn't get the best grades in school, but that's because the teachers didn't understand him."

"It's too hot outside, I don't want to go for a walk," said the daughter.

"How hot can it be? Just a short walk. We're not asking you to go harvest the rice plants," muttered her mother, giving her daughter a push.

Outside, the daughter walked alone with Jujube Lou. Whenever she stole a glance at his face, she found his eyes focused on her chest.

Awkwardly, they circled around the residential compound, where some old folks sat in the shade, talking, watching babies. She knew it was what her mother wanted, for her to notice these things. That was family life, after all: married, grandparents, kids, an apartment in a family compound with friendly guards at the gates, old trees growing between the paved paths.

The daughter watched a baby waddling in its crotchless pants. A wrinkled grandmother picked up another toddler and held it facing outwards, legs spread. A stream of urine jetted out onto a patch of dead grass.

She looked at Jujube Lou, wondering if he had noticed. He was still fixated on her chest, but he looked up and met her eyes. His expression wasn't sympathy or understanding, but a sort of dull innocence.

A moment later, the boy sneezed and began wiping his nose with his shirt.

"Excuse me, it's really too hot outside," the daughter said, before hurrying back.

"What happened?" Aunt Lou said, upon their arrival. Aunt Lou looked at her son. "He's just feeling a little sick."

This was welcome news for the daughter. "But it's not even winter. I don't want someone who is just more trouble to take care of."

The two parents listened, dismayed.

"He's a good guy, just wait until he recovers," said Aunt Lou. "It's nothing serious, just a small cold."

The daughter didn't have any special feelings for him and didn't care to be kind. To defend herself, she was willing to use any reason.

"I don't want a man who gets sick easily. He won't be able to keep a good job and help with the house chores, let alone care for a baby." Jujube Lou stood with his face down, snot running down to his mouth. "How come no other girl has married him? There's something not right, I can tell that after just a few minutes."

Afterward, the daughter and her mother walked back to their apartment. The mother shook her head. "How could you speak like that? You're just coming up with reasons why he's not right. Why don't you want to get married?"

"I do, but just not to him."

"He's as good as anyone else. Tell me, what is it? You want to shop around first?"

The term *shop around* made the daughter uncomfortable. It wasn't how she would describe it, but it wasn't too far from the truth. She wanted to experiment, to have a different life, perhaps do something ridiculous. But what *ridiculous* really meant was beyond her fingertips, just at the tip of her tongue.

In a way, she felt sorry for her mother. She knew her mother loved and cared for her, and only wanted the best outcome. If only she could put a name to this affliction, this emptiness in her heart, she would feel better. She wanted something so different from this life that had been planned for her. "I can't stand it," she said, through clenched teeth. She began to run away from her mother.

The mother reached out and grabbed her shoulder. "We'll go downtown, People's Square, and visit the marriage market. After you have a look around, you'll feel better about marrying Aunt Lou's son. Wear something nice for a change, the new dress I bought you, that pink-and-white one with the stripes."

It was a generous compromise.

It was past noon by the time they got there. People's Square was across the road. On the left side was an old mall with a Xinhua Bookstore on three floors with books of every kind: *Mao Zedong Complete Works, Deng Xiaoping Thought,* two large sections of educational material on English. On the right was a KFC, and farther down was the city park and fashion district.

The marriage market was not exactly in the public square, but in the park adjacent. As for the park, there wasn't much grass, only a few trees, and on every side were honking cars. The air was not too good. In fact, it was quite bad. But the park was large and open to the public. People met for constructive civic activities like square dancing, the marriage market and walking pets and children.

Outside the gate of the park were a few food vendors, like a Taiwanese waffle maker, and a fragrant-tea seller. There were upscale shops too, even a new Häagen-Dazs, except the sign was being redone because of the wrong spelling.

Inside the park they walked with trees shading the sun. Still, it was so bright the daughter took out her hat, a cool fashionable visor. The visor was so eye-catching and expensive-looking that the mother noticed it. "Where'd you get that?" she asked.

"My boyfriend gave it to me," the daughter said. "He's the one that works in a hat shop. It's not a bad job, and he's handsome."

"A hat shop? How much can he make in a year? Is he even a local? Does he have an apartment in Suzhou? A car? Who can he support with a hat shop? I'm your mother, what do you know about men? A stupid girl like you will fall in love with the first boy who looks in your direction."

It was pleasant in the park, but the daughter dragged her feet. "Why are you walking like that? Pick your feet up."

The daughter coughed and cleared her throat. "I have a headache."

"You're just pretending. Stand upright, like a lady."

Behind her mother's back, the daughter mimicked her mother's facial expressions. Her mother caught her.

"What kind of ungrateful daughter are you? I'm doing all this for you. Show some respect. Why wear such a nice dress if you're going to slouch and grumble like that?"

"Fine, okay," the daughter said, straightening her back.

"I'm sure we can find a man we can both agree on." The mother looked around the park, from one side to the other, seeming happier.

On each side of the paved path were groups of mothers and aunties, grandmothers and uncles. Some crouched in the shade by the bushes, others fanned themselves under the sun. Rows of flyers and posters were on display, featuring photos and information about sons and daughters. The mother and daughter walked up to take a closer look. The mother held her daughter close by the arm. Amid the chatter and laughter, the daughter thought, *I'll try not to be so difficult. I'll try to open up. If I force myself to smile, I'll enjoy it.*

Standing in the park, amid the crowds, she spotted someone she thought she recognized, an old school chum. "Hey, there's someone I know – Ling."

This Ling was a delightful girl, whom the daughter liked. Ling had talked to her a lot, been a good listener. They had once even skipped a class together and hid behind the school wall where Ling told her about what it meant to "get in bed." When the daughter was alone later that day, she locked herself in the bathroom, took off her clothes and stared at the reflection in the mirror above the sink. She touched herself. The skin on her body was hot under her fingers. This was how she would feel, maybe, to someone else.

But, in the park, when the familiar person turned around, the daughter saw it was only an old aunty with a wrinkled face.

"You're pretty, my dear," the aunty said. "How old are you?"

"She's my daughter, just the right age to marry."

"How lovely. I have a son who's a good match. He's unmarried, and I think he'd be perfect." The aunty held up the piece of paper in her hands. She had been holding it for the whole day and there were stains on its creased surface. The daughter could make out the black-and-white photo of a round man with a balding head, wearing spectacles.

"Where is your family from?" asked the mother.

"Wuxi originally, but we live in Suzhou now. My son is a floor manager for a company that sells American milk powder. You see, he has an executive salary. In the future, if my son has a baby, the baby will have all the imported milk powder it needs. Isn't that something?"

The aunty made a good point: milk products were not easy to find. It wasn't that the daughter had a child to look after, but one day, when she did, she would want it to have the best.

There were opportunities all around. But the daughter wasn't interested in the photo the woman was holding. All the son's statistics were listed on the flyer: his monthly wages, his measurements, his hobbies and employment history, his education and test scores.

The daughter watched as her mother carefully examined the data. Would the daughter finally appreciate her mother's due diligence? Could she for once give her mother the credit that was due? The daughter tried to care, to feel moved by her mother's concern and effort, but the feeling was more like a rock turning and turning in her stomach. Trying to hide her boredom and discomfort, the daughter stepped back and glanced farther down the path.

"How come he's not married?" the mother asked. Her blunt tone was insulting, but the aunty took no offence.

"He almost did once. He had a woman, but she turned out to be a rotten two-timer. He wasted a year on her, and spent lots of money. But I want to know more about your daughter."

"Well, you can see for yourself that she's a pretty thing. She has an education too – we put a lot of money into her. To be honest, she's a bit spoiled, but children these days, which of them isn't? They don't know how to be grateful."

The mother listed all her daughter's details, years of education, strengths in school, the kind of food her daughter liked, where she worked and so on. "Stand up straight," she said, slapping her daughter on the back. Her daughter pulled her shoulder blades back and her chest jutted out a little. The mother was right, her daughter needed all the help she could get, especially with that small bosom.

"Like I said, she's a bit uppity. You just have to remind her every now and then, and she'll come around. She didn't even want to come today. But now that she's here, she's cooperating well."

"She's tall enough," replied the aunty.

The daughter pondered her life. Everyone knew that her younger brother would be expensive: his schooling, his future bride. The daughter's marriage would mean money for the family, much-needed relief from the pressures of the modern economy. Wasn't it a fair exchange? Her bad behaviour was pointless.

"Let's exchange WeChat contacts. We can arrange a time for them to meet."

There didn't seem to be any order to the activity. Some people had flyers showing off their sons. Other people's flyers featured daughters. Some photos were in faded black and white, like mug shots; others were in full colour with photo finish. The detailed lists of information accompanying each picture made the daughter's head spin.

The mother pulled her from one flyer to the next. "That boy wasn't so bad. What did you think?"

Together the mother and daughter sat down in the shade of a tree. Her mother smacked her on the shoulder. "Pay attention when I'm talking, daughter. Come on, which one do you like?" Her mother had taken snapshots of flyers on her phone and together they reviewed them, swiping from one to the next.

All the faces seemed to blur together. All had the same white-collared dress shirt; short black hair; black eyes; a forced, fake smile. Some were taller, some shorter, fatter or thinner, wore eyeglasses or didn't. To the daughter, it was all the same boring thing. *Perhaps I'm not the only one who is so bored of this*, she thought.

The daughter looked at her mother, who let out a long, exasperated sigh. "All this way for nothing," said the mother. "Why should a mother tire herself out when her daughter doesn't even appreciate it?"

"I'm sorry, I really am."

"What do you want? Just tell me, why are you being so troublesome?"

Her mother's voice was so sincere, so exhausted, the daughter felt guilty. She wanted to answer truthfully, but all she could say was, "I want someone different."

"So stupid." The mother shook her head. "What did I do to have an impossible daughter like you?"

The footpath that snaked past where they were sitting ended twenty metres away at an open paved space. The black and white stones were arranged in a yin and yang pattern, common enough in parks. A couple dozen young people were gathered there. A tall, lanky man in a cheap suit waved a bullhorn, with a boom box by his feet. Sets of aunties and a few uncles sat or stood off to the side.

"Let's see what's happening over there," the mother said.

"I'm tired. Let's go home."

"We're already here." The mother pulled her daughter along. "Why do you insist on being so difficult?"

The crowd of young people had organized themselves into two circles, according to gender. Women on the inside, men on the outside. Presently the man with the bullhorn blew a whistle and began playing music from the speaker system. The men started walking so that the male circle rotated around the female circle. The whistle was blown again. The music stopped, as did the men. Each man was now paired with a young woman, and the new couples nervously chatted with each other.

It was a good matchmaking activity. However, at a glance, the daughter could see all the men standing there, and none of them caught her eye.

"That's fun and useful," said the mother. "Go and join them."

"I don't think so. I want to meet someone on my own."

The mother shook her head and sighed. They were about to leave, when the daughter took one last look at the circle. One of the women was standing on the curving line between the white and black paved stones. The woman was tall and beautiful with a short, black pixie cut, side-swept bangs, a lovely straight nose and a wide mouth.

The daughter took a step forward without even thinking. A cool breeze carried a scent under her nose, smelling of ripe apricots and peaches. She looked at her mother.

"Okay," she said, "I'll try it."

2.
The City

DURING THE FIRST WEEK OF SCHOOL, I WENT WITH A CLASS-
mate, a young student from Japan, to shoot some pool. At that
time I could hardly communicate with anyone, him least of all.
We played a couple of games, but because the place was so smoky,
we left early.

On our way back we passed a shoddy plaza. One of the shops
sold finger traps and fortune cookies, something I had never seen
before. Weren't fortune cookies an American invention, a sort of
edible, colonial neologism? Taped to the windowpane was a handwritten Help Wanted sign.

We went inside – the shop was brightly lit and the red-uni-
formed staff were courteous and well trained. I found the person in charge, a young woman of a rather sickly pale complexion,
who wore her hair in a ponytail. She had an odd shape about her:
every limb on her body was short and pudgy, but her body was
the opposite, long and narrow. I took an immediate liking to her
because of the way she smiled. She had a toothy, goofy smile, with

huge canine-like incisors, which she sometimes covered with her hand when she giggled.

She introduced herself as the accountant and manager.

"My – name – Danny – I – am – looking – for – job," I said, as best as I could. My Japanese classmate was amused and tried to help by translating for me. However, he seemed to be just as hopeless a speaker as I was.

"But you can't even speak Chinese, how can you have a job here?" asked the young accountant.

"I – can – speak. I – can – improve."

She must have thought I was cute, because we sat down and, though we could hardly communicate, she fussed over me like a mother.

"Why do you need a job? Do you live at the university? Do you want a cup of hot water?" She presented a form that I filled out with my personal details. I hoped she would get my contact info from the form and contact me, and I waited for a few days, but she didn't.

A week later I dropped by the shop again. I didn't care about the form and the job, as she must have known; I just wanted to see her.

"I'm working," she said, from her tiny closet office. Somehow, I managed to convince her to come outside on her break.

"The weather is really nice outside."

"I'm busy, sorry."

"I don't mind waiting. Do you get a break soon?"

"In fifteen minutes."

"Why don't I wait outside for you then."

"Shouldn't you be in class, though?"

"I finished early today."

"I can't go anywhere, even on break."

"You can stand outside your shop, can't you?"

"Yeah, okay."

We sat on a bench, not on the seat, because it was so dusty and dirty, but on the back rail of it. Every evening, I came over to find her after work, and it turned into a routine and we became friends. We sat like that, talking, until the summer passed and it was too cold.

"I don't know why the other international students like living on campus," I told her. "We all came here to learn Chinese. Every day we go to class and the only person who can speak Chinese is the teacher. That's why I moved off-campus. I want to have friends like you."

I had a first-floor room on my own, it was true, in a residential compound not far from the school. Actually, it was a two-bedroom place and the landlord lived in the master bedroom, while I occupied a tiny spare room that had a broken window. The place crawled with insects – cockroaches and horrid red millipedes that were impossible to kill. I liked my room because it was right in the middle of the neighbourhood, where the real living happened. And, of course, I liked it because it was within my budget.

The young accountant got into the habit of visiting me after work. She would stand outside my window and plaintively say my name, repeating it until I answered her.

"Dan-ny, Dan-ny? Dan-ny Woo?"

She spoke in a low voice, urgent and annoyed if I took too long. I would hurry out, opening the front door. She would slip quickly into my room.

"Don't you think these textbooks are too hard?" she asked.

I was auditing a third-year course, and I had been in the country only a month. The baokan textbook I had bought was already covered with notes. I was studying Mandarin Chinese, taking a variety of speaking and writing courses. The baokan class was the hardest, a course on reading newspapers.

"This way I'll learn faster," I told her.

In between studying, we talked. She had first come to Beijing from a village a couple of hours away. Each year, during holidays, she would take the bus home to her village, and each time she would be sick from the bus ride, she said. Later, when she returned from Spring Festival, I was shocked to see how unwell she looked, and indeed, she needed a week to recover. It was the trip that she couldn't stand, the queasiness and motion sickness.

Life in her village, on the other hand, must have been a different world altogether. I could detect traces of it in her traditional, conservative philosophy of life. Whenever I made an overture of affection, for example, she would be perplexed, unable to respond other than to rebuff me awkwardly.

Sometimes I would open the door for her and slip back under the covers in bed. My room was such a mess, she would have nowhere to sit except for the edge of the uncomfortable mattress, next to me. Like that, with her back to me, we would talk for an hour. If she felt the accidental pressure of my body through the covers, she would stand up, still talking with her back to me, loitering awkwardly as though she hadn't noticed.

As for the landlord, he was her complete opposite. He was five foot five and would stand in a pair of black Speedos by my door, arm fully extended, pointing his finger at my nose, demanding more money. His trademark move was to step back and shadow kick the air near my crotch. Whenever he got too animated, he would shout in his angry, operatic voice that I had "no balls" and ask rhetorically, "Aren't you a man? Aren't you? You're not a man, you've got no balls." He had a way of slamming the front door, which was right outside my room, by spinning around, his foot kicking the door shut with a loud bang. During the day, if he was around, I would see him standing by the street, leering at passersby, his sweat-soaked shirt rolled up.

He liked putting the tip of his index finger on his own nose when he wanted to emphasize himself. There was an old laundry machine in the closet of his dark, cluttered apartment. One day I was tired of handwashing my clothes and asked to try it.

"I don't want to catch your germs," he shouted, pointing his finger at his nose. "Look at my back." He pulled his shirt up to show me the black dots on his back. "The previous tenant used it and look what happened. Don't you dare use it, you filthy animal."

Whenever my friend visited, he would hound her. One day she came over while I was out.

"You again?" he said.

"I'll wait outside."

"We all know what you're doing here, you little tramp."

"I am not doing anything. He's my friend. His Chinese needs improvement."

"You think I'm that dumb?" asked the landlord. "The security guards see you coming over every day. You have no shame, you're depraved, practically a prostitute." The landlord spat on the ground.

"I never did anything dishonourable," she said. She was crying when I arrived. She ran by me, down the street, toward her shop. I didn't know what had happened, but I chased after her.

"What's going on? What's wrong?" It took half an hour for her to calm down enough that she could tell me what happened.

"Don't listen to that guy," I said. "I need to find a new place to live."

From then on, I went over to her fortune cookie shop more. I got in the habit of buying the cookie scraps – these were pieces of cookies that had been broken or destroyed somehow. They were collected and put into transparent plastic gift bags and sold at discounted prices. With just a few coins I could purchase a big bag of these. My friend would watch me eating from this bag of scraps and giggle, covering her mouth and her incisors.

As the accountant and manager, she was responsible for coming up with the fortunes. I read them and rolled my eyes. They had all the classics, like "You will become so famous" and "You will find true love soon."

"These are so unoriginal," I said.

"If you can think of some better ones, write them down." But when I sat down to write a few fortunes, I didn't feel any inspiration. I wrote a few that I thought were not too bad, but the accountant didn't like them:

"Others will soon appreciate your hygienic standards."

"Eat less and you will become richer."

"Try yelling when people cannot hear you."

The landlord got worse. One day he opened my door, peeling a cucumber. "Here," he said, holding the half-peeled cucumber up to my face, "I bought this for you." I knew he was up to no good, and I ignored him. That night, however, I woke up to a strange noise. After checking the door, and seeing no one was there, I sat back on my bed.

I had a hot water bottle and poured myself a cup, sipping the water. It was lukewarm, but there was a funny taste. I unscrewed the lid and looked in. There was the peeled cucumber, looking yellowish and slimy, as if it had been dipped in the toilet.

It was so revolting, I threw up and spent the next day in bed, unable to eat anything at all. When I recovered, I moved into the school dormitory while I looked for a better place off-campus. I received a stream of threatening text messages from the landlord, each one making me more nervous.

Where are you?

Where have you moved?? I'm waiting for you!

I have something for you!!!

Why am I so misfortunate to have met you?! You deserve to die!

There's a fire. Come now and get your things!

You're a dead dog, I'll kill you soon!!!

When I went to pick up my things from his apartment, I found all my stuff in a pile on the pavement outside my window, half of it missing.

He came out of his apartment a moment after I arrived. At first he was furious, dancing around me with anger. Then, after yelling for a few minutes, he quieted down as I began to gather up my belongings.

"Where have you been?"

"I moved. I've been living somewhere else."

"You moved into the school, didn't you?" I shrugged, not wanting to say much. "I know you've been living in the school. I went there looking for you, but they wouldn't tell me which room you were in. Did they tell you I was there?" I shook my head, keeping a tight lip.

"I had no idea," I said. It was an honest answer.

"I shouted at them, I made a huge scene, but they refused to talk to me. I told them what a bum, a dog, a scoundrel you were, but they wouldn't help me out." He went on, complaining about how the concierge had treated him in the foreign student hotel.

"A guy like you, barging into a place like that, what did you expect them to do?" I said, surprised at how hurt he was.

"Are you sure you don't want to stay? I'll give you a good deal for the next year." I shook my head and he began yelling at me again before kicking at my pile of clothes and towels. They fanned out into the road, and he laughed as they were run over.

After moving to the school dorm, I was still looking for a new, more permanent place to rent. One day I asked a young security guard near the finger trap and fortune cookie shop.

"My uncle and aunt have a room," he said. "They're right across the street."

He led me to a peaceful six-floor residential compound, crowded with families and quite old. The surrounding area was systematically being torn down and replaced with newer buildings, as everything seemed to be in that city. The unit was on the first floor, opening out to a restaurant parking lot. The yard was littered with trash that had been thrown out of the apartments above. The front door of every household was plastered with stickers advertising all kinds of services: locksmithing, water pipe fixing, electrician shops, rush-to-your-door service.

A family occupied the railroad-style home. A mother and father, a grandmother who had to be at least ninety years old and deaf, and the twenty-five-year-old son who had graduated from school and played video games all day. His fiancée slept in his bed and constantly cried. Everywhere were cats and dogs running about, over a dozen of them. I couldn't keep track of them all.

I liked living there. I liked the crassness of the family and the grimy, raw, unfiltered home life. They were loud and had awful manners, but they were friendly, maybe because I was paying rent. The mother wore her sleeping gown all day and squatted in front of an enormous flat-screen TV hanging on the wall of the unpainted living room. She would pull out a bedpan and relieve herself right there instead of using the closet toilet, not taking her eyes off the TV. She liked to watch many shows, one of which I remember called *Fei Chang Wu Rao*, a contestant dating show in which a bachelor vied for the affection of a dozen charming women.

"Don't pick that one," she said, at the TV bachelor. "She looks like a yellow snake. You can do better." The next contestant came on, a thin man wearing a brightly coloured three-piece suit. "Look at this guy, this Comrade Fudgepacker. Where are the respectable gents?"

In a loud voice, I exclaimed, "He seems pretty respectable to me!"

She stared. "You should be on this show. The girls would love you."

Before bed, I got into the habit of brushing my teeth in the kitchen. The closet toilet was such a horrid place – so cramped one could not enter without rubbing against the dark, moist lip of the seatless toilet bowl – I used it as seldom as possible. One evening the kitchen sink, which drained into a concrete basin on the floor, got clogged. Thinking I had caused the problem, I took the plunger from the bathroom.

"Let me do that," the mother said.

"It's probably my fault. The suds from my tooth-brushing probably caused it."

"No, it happens all the time."

In her nightgown and rubber sandals, she thrust the plunger in the basin, sloshing the water back and forth, until she was soaked in sweat and the floor was slick. It was backbreaking work that went on for half an hour. The whole time, a cigarette dangled from her mouth. I watched her, feeling quite bad.

"I'll give it a go."

"You?" she wheezed. "What can you do? You've got twigs for legs and arms. Go read a book."

From the doorway, the father and son watched as well, arms folded over their chests, grunting now and again at her effort.

The family chain-smoked, the mother worst of all. She started smoking at seven in the morning and smoked through as many packs as she could during the day right until she went to sleep. She would hold a cigarette between her fingers in one hand, and pick up dog poop with the other, bare hand.

The worst offender was a small terrier who, perhaps because he was fond of me, made a habit of pooping directly in the middle of my doorway. More than once I opened the door to find him doing his business, and he would thump his tiny tail, as if for my approval. From time to time, returning from an outing, I found this dog on the opposite side of the street, too scared to cross because of the busy road. I would pick him up and carry him across, and he would lick my face a dozen times before I could put him down.

Inside their apartment, the living room always smelled of smoke, and raw meat sat in piles in the corner until the mother decided it was time to cook it. A stray cat tortured birds under the square table that was used for dinner and mah-jong. At night, I saw a cat and dog mating – the terrier that licked my face. Whenever I caught them, they would freeze in the act and look up at me with guilty eyes.

After school, I often came home to find the grandmother sitting on my bed, staring off into space. I sat, ate and did my homework at my desk, with her lying inches from me, neither of us saying a word.

Sometimes there were appalling fights between the fiancée on one side, and the mother and son on the other, who constantly aggravated her. Once I locked my bedroom door when I heard plates crashing. I knew from the yelling that the fiancée had grabbed a kitchen knife to defend herself. It was such a grim scene, but I didn't have the courage to open my door and intervene. The fiancée left that evening and the next day the mother and son knocked on my door.

"We kicked out that no-good woman. Can you take my son to the school to find him a pretty girl? He's a good guy." The son stood there, patting the hair on his oily head.

"He's a filmmaker," the mother explained.

"I want to recruit some sexy girls for a movie I'm making." He nodded, as if this was something I would know about.

One afternoon I came back to find some of my belongings missing. I didn't mind, but I had an expensive sports racquet that was gone.

"We sold them," said the mother, apologetically. "Did you want those things?"

Despite all that, I liked them and got along with them, if only because they were so much better than my previous landlord. At least they did not bother me about who I had over, and the young accountant enjoyed visiting. Like before, she would stand outside, calling my name until I opened the door for her.

"Dan-ny Woo," I would hear, in a timid, urgent voice. "Dan-ny Woo?" She would go on like that for ten minutes, unless I went out to get her. She had a broken, cheap phone that she never used, because she paid by the minute.

A few times a week, I would visit her in her dorm. Or rather, more often, I would follow her there after work. Her dorm was across the street from the plaza, at the back of a residential complex, where there was a little shack with a stairwell leading down into a set of tenements deep underground.

The first few times, the young accountant had to show me the way to her room through the winding corridors. There was only one exit, but without her I would get lost. We passed many doors, where the residents sat close to the floor, cooking over little hot plates or scrubbing dirty underwear in plastic tubs. Here and there the dim, harsh light of the corridors would go dark. The ghastly tiled floors became bare black concrete or packed dirt, and the path was blocked by monstrous iron gates, tangled in barbed wire, barricaded by miscellaneous trash. Behind the gates one could see the tunnel stretch on and on, disappearing into darkness. The underground residence, the tunnels, had been constructed as emergency bomb shelters during the war with Japan years ago. They crisscrossed underneath the entire city. Now many of them had been repurposed as cheap housing.

Tucked away in a dark, slimy corner, she showed me a tiny spiral staircase, so narrow and tight I had to hold my breath to pass up through it. It took minutes to ascend to the top, and whenever I went up, I would have to fight spasms of panic and claustrophobia. I would wave my hand inches from my eyes and see nothing, not knowing if my eyes were open or closed.

"We share this floor with another shop," I heard the young accountant's voice say. "The employees of a bakery live down that hallway, and we live over in that hallway." She was in front of me, and I could feel the movement of air from her breath.

I turned on my phone's torch. The darkness was such that the light was swallowed up. Later on, I borrowed a large flashlight and explored the place. We were in a large cavern, with two bombed-out elevator shafts at one end, the doors gone. One misstep, and anyone could fall down into the abyss.

* * *

All that week there had been news coverage of anti-Japanese rioting, a territorial dispute in the South China Sea involving the Diaoyu Islands. Several Japanese stores in the city had been smashed. One of my classmates, Miriko, sat in class directly behind me. She had been a little quieter than usual, and lowered her head, her hair falling over her face, whenever conversation turned to the angry riots. She was from Hiroshima and was taller than me. From below, my eyes always focused on her right ear, which was cleft and misshapen.

On a whim I turned to her. "Are you busy this afternoon? Want to come visit my friend?"

"Are you sure it's safe?"

"I think it's quite safe. It's not far, we can walk. You'll see."

Four Japanese students came, including Miriko. My accountant friend met us at her fortune cookie shop, where I introduced them.

"You don't mind, do you?" I asked the accountant.

"Of course not."

"With everything that's been going on in the news about the rioting, taking her on an outing might make her feel better."

"You're right. She'll see a part of the city she probably doesn't know exists."

The accountant beamed. She led the way to her dorm, smiling her goofy, toothy smile, clasping her hands together. Though they couldn't communicate in any language, they seemed to understand each other.

We followed the accountant across the road, through the parking lot, down the stairs, through the winding corridors, up the nightmarish staircase, through the dark cavern and into the set of horrid rooms, full of stale-smelling clothes, body odour and old food.

As we walked, the accountant asked me about Miriko.

"She's been feeling unwell this whole week," I said. "It's the riots, it's everything. I don't know."

"Where's she from?" the accountant asked. "What city?"

"Hiroshima."

She gave me a serious look, but I could only stare blankly ahead.

I wondered if I had made a mistake bringing them here. When I looked, the sombre, awed faces of my classmates worried me. Miriko sat down on the accountant's bed, the lower bunk, and stared at the room.

The light in the room was a dim, electric blue, like pale-blue tinfoil. Pipes wrapped in newspaper or plastic shopping bags ran through the room at strange places, entering gaping black holes in the wall. A series of deflated, dirty balloons – so horrible-looking they might as well have been used condoms – hung from a string from one pipe to another. In the middle of the room was a little table, with rice bowls, shampoo, soap and half-eaten food. Beetles with golden wings crawled over everything. Under some beds were brightly coloured plastic tubs used for washing. There was no running hot water in the communal bathroom, and the residents had to get their hot water from a steel water boiler.

The young accountant sat down next to Miriko. For a long time they sat there together.

"Want to play a game?" I asked.

I kept some of my personal belongings underneath the accountant's bed in a cardboard box. I pulled it out and set it on the bed, when I had a strange feeling.

"What are you guys doing?" I said. "Why are you so quiet?" They were sitting so close together, their knees touching. I looked at them and laughed nervously. "Are you okay? What's wrong?" My accountant friend shook her head. They both smiled a bit too, embarrassed.

"Nothing, nothing," the accountant said, wiping her face. Miriko wiped her own, like a reflection in a mirror.

"Why are you guys crying?" I didn't get an answer. They only shielded their faces from me.

I slipped quietly into the next room and waited with my other classmates. In the silence, I heard someone, either Miriko or the accountant, blowing her nose. When I peered in, they were standing up, smoothing out the sheet on the bunk bed.

"We're ready to go back out."

I was too. Ready to walk through the tunnels again, up to the street.

Sometimes I would go for walks by myself. I liked parks, but there was only one park nearby. To get there, I walked through a bunch of back alleys. This was an older part of the city, and every block was undergoing some kind of construction. Entire swaths were being developed. The density and volume of infrastructure was difficult for me to comprehend – it was tall and wide and noisy and fast. One day I rode my bike down an alley just minutes from where I lived, turned a corner and found an enormous empty eight-lane road, brand new, the tar still cooling. It went on and on, curving out of sight, with buildings squished on either side of it.

I only had to turn my head to see shanties with corrugated roofing, decaying bricks and old, dried aunties beating and sunning their blankets and rugs. In colder months, in the alleys, by the river and the outdoor market, people would gather around steel drums, warming themselves with fire. Day and night, crowds of men would face off over chessboards, the wooden disc-shaped pieces identical except for the characters engraved on them. Here, I often stopped to chat with the vendors who sold roasted sweet potatoes, which lined the insides of the drums. Those sweet potatoes were my favourite snack; I liked the soft, warm orange insides, and the rough skin, which oozed sap. After pointing to my choice through the opening of the drum, the vendor would carefully take it out and hang it from a metal rod to calculate its weight and cost.

Cutting through the area was a murky river with a tiny footbridge for bicycles and people going to the market. Along the banks, fishermen spent hours trying to catch tiny fish. I liked these places most; the paths were too narrow for cars. Such an abundance of food carts, hawkers and old aunties and uncles thrived here. In the middle of it all sat a squat woman, her face wrinkled and red, bundled in ratty cloths, at a pedal-operated sewing machine. I often had her do my sewing, but what language she spoke and where she had come from was a complete mystery. The sounds she made were incomprehensible to me. No matter what I asked her to do, the fee was always the same, one yuan, or at most two.

From that footbridge one could see the park, and a classical, dynastic pagoda, eight-sided, that was centuries old. I spent whole afternoons wandering around that park. People would come hang their birdcages in the trees. Other than the caged pet birds, the place was nearly devoid of wildlife.

Opposite the pagoda was a shallow pool, frozen over in winter. In warmer seasons, one could see minnows darting about like black pixies. I often saw a chubby boy with rusty red cheeks holding an empty water bottle. He had a fishnet he used for catching minnows. I would stand too, looking over his shoulder, mesmerized by the shadows.

On the far side of the park was an old locomotive and railcar, aged and firebombed, oriented to appear like it was coasting out of a gathering of trees. In the ground were craters, the remnants of unfinished excavations, where children often played games.

One day the young accountant came with me.

"Has that train always been there?" I asked.

"I don't see how it could be. It was probably left there, destroyed during the war."

We talked to a man in a guard uniform, sitting idly by the river, with a fishing pole.

"They get smaller every year," he said, shaking his head. He spanned his thumb and pinky, showing me the biggest fish he had caught.

"Do you sell them or eat them?"

"Eat them," he said.

I looked at the murky water. "Are they safe to eat?"

"Safe? Why not?" He recited a recipe for fish congee. At the end of his line a fish splashed out of the water.

"That was a good recipe," the accountant said.

Coming back from the park we cut through an old cobblestone path, with single-storey shanties on either side. Naked children peed on the brick walls, the urine turning golden dust to wet, black stains. We walked past the ruined shanties, workmen with pickaxes standing on mounds of rubble. They all wore helmets. A man came out to talk to us, with a burnt brown face, wearing a mein lap. A small child stood at his feet fidgeting. "Our dog will bite you," the boy said, as we walked away. The boy shouted after us, "How did you find us here?"

At the end of the cobblestone path, there was a field of rubble, demolished ping fangs, one-storey houses razed to the ground. The field ended on all sides, giving way to more one-storey houses, people going about their lives. Every week the field got bigger.

Whenever we went for a walk, the young accountant had a habit of lagging behind me. I would be walking and talking, with her next to me. After a few minutes she would be a step or two behind. It didn't matter how slowly I walked.

"Why do you keep doing that?" I said.

"What?"

She pretended not to know what she was doing. If I didn't bother her about it, she would end up directly behind me, following like I had her on a leash.

When she stopped to talk to a stranger, she would say something like, "Ah, uncle," or "Excuse me, big sister," or "Hey, brother."

They would always reply, always meet her gaze and smile. She had an open face, I guess, like she would accept anyone who came her way, without questions.

For a while, because I wanted to be closer to her, I moved in with the young accountant. Not in her dorm with all the fortune cookie shop's employees, but in a small room on the lower level of the underground residence, as near the exit as possible. My room wasn't too far from the communal bathroom, whose stench, worst in the evenings, wafted over day and night.

I felt right at home down there, underneath BeiWa Road, with the entire city above me. My subterranean neighbours were from every part of China, except Beijing. They had all come to find work. Some stayed a week. Others settled and made homes down there, raising children.

I liked my room too, which had nothing but a metal cot in the middle, with a foot of elbow space on either side and a light bulb dangling from the ceiling. The door, a flimsy piece of cork, had a hole in the wall above it, for ventilation. Like all the other rooms in that place, there was a large, unsightly pipe running across the ceiling and down one corner.

Perhaps I felt at home because of the silence. I loved that kind of silence, in the middle of the city, two storeys underground, in a labyrinth. One afternoon, bored, I sang a few songs from *Les Misérables*, lying on my cot, facing the ceiling. My voice, normally reedy and weak, boomed out, echoing down the halls. After about ten minutes, I noticed someone was calling my name outside my door.

"Danny?" said the young accountant, in an urgent voice. "Dan-ny Woo?" I opened the door and beckoned her in.

Like always, the accountant never knocked. I could never get her to explain why. She was afraid she would find me with a woman, perhaps, or worse.

"What are you doing? I didn't know you were a talented singer."

"I'm not, but the walls make me sound good."

She sat on my cot, coughing. Everyone who lived down there had a chronic cough. Maybe it was the air in people's lungs, tickling people's throats. I got used to it, the sound of people coughing, like I got used to the cockroaches.

"If you washed your hair, you'd be very good-looking," the young accountant said. "Why do you do that?"

"Do what?"

She wore clothes as shabby as mine. There was only one shower, above ground, attached to the entrance shack. Neither one of us used it often, but at least the young accountant washed her hair.

"It's starting to stick together; you've got a bun on your head." She nodded to it. "I've never seen hair like that before."

"I don't want to waste water. It's called a dreadlock, but it's not a loc, it's more like a dreadball."

"People ask me if you're homeless. I told them you're a student."

"Not much difference."

"You should get your pants fixed too." She pointed to the fraying hem of my pants. "There's a woman by the river who does it, I'll show you."

I didn't bother telling her that I already knew this woman, and when the accountant led me there, the woman, in her language neither of us understood, betrayed nothing.

I could put up with the sound of people coughing. Worse were fireworks. Whenever there was a holiday or wedding, or the opening of a store, there was terrible noise. Cased in belts of colourful paper like ammunition, they made terrific bangs and set off the alarm bells of nearby scooters and cars, a chain reaction that lasted for hours. People were so gleeful at leaving red confetti everywhere, I couldn't understand it. Underground, I could escape the sound.

Later, during festivals, I saw happy children cradling armloads of fireworks, a sparkler burning in one hand. What I liked most was the day after, when it looked like drifts of burnt rose petals had been swept into every corner of the city, gloriously red and pink and gold.

At dinner, the fortune cookie shop's cook treated me to meals. He was a skinny man, always cursing. His cooking station was at the entrance shack above ground, opposite the shower stall. I would get in line with the others.

"Xiao huo zi, how about dinner, eh?"

"Thank you, but you're too generous," I said.

He strode up and spat on the floor in front of me, wiping his face with the back of his hand. "Come, have dinner, it's nothing at all. Look how much food there is."

He gestured to a walk-in closet with sacks of potatoes, vegetables, rice. The sacks were clear plastic, leaving nothing to the imagination. The cookware was oversized, as big as a witch's cauldron. The shop's employees showed up in threes and fours. Everyone brought their own utensils and reusable containers.

After getting food, I went with the young accountant back down to her dorm room, where we ate. There were no chairs, so I sat on her low bunk while she crouched on the clay floor.

One day at school I got in the elevator together with a Japanese classmate; we were speaking in English. The elevator was already crowded and beside me stood an American exchange student, tall and blond, whom I had never met. She turned to me and smiled.

"Back home I had a friend like you," she said.

"Oh, thank you." I pushed my eyeglasses up my nose, not knowing what else to say.

The foreigners' dormitory was a hotel, the flagship building of the school, featured on the cover of all its brochures. At the top, in mid-air, was an enormous indoor skywalk connecting the dormitory to the classrooms, so that we didn't have to go outside to get to our classes. Lining this large hallway were desks and chairs where foreign students often sat, and where I would sometimes study.

It was a popular spot. On a sunny afternoon an attractive young Chinese woman, a senior, or grad student perhaps, walked by and waved to me. I had spoken to her only once before, trying to be friendly with her, but she had snubbed me. I was surprised, flattered that she would come talk to me where I sat studying.

"Hi, you," she said, smiling and being inexplicably friendly. I said a word or two in English, trying to contain my excitement, when she turned to the man sitting beside me, a young white man, a student on an exchange program from North Carolina, as it turned out. "Is this your friend?" she asked me. She was already looking at him and shook his hand. They laughed, talked and exchanged phone numbers. She waved and left without looking at me again.

The handsome guy grinned at me. I had been sitting beside him for some time, each of us studying quietly. "Oh, you surprised me. I didn't know you could speak English."

"Yeah." I bit my lip and looked back down at my book.

A few weeks later, the accountant needed to print new labels because the prices of fortune cookies had gone up but the label maker was malfunctioning. None of the cookie makers or finger trap artisans knew how to fix it.

I had no technical computer background, but she asked me to take a look. Her office, the only room in the store with a door, was big enough for just her computer, the label maker and a chair. I knew enough to see that the operating system was Windows but the language was in Chinese. Everything looked unfamiliar.

"Where are the printer options?"

"I don't know." She shrugged. "What's that?"

She went about her business, as if she knew it was only a matter of time before I fixed the problem. It was a fluke, but I managed to find the dialogue box I was looking for. All I knew was something about the ports, so I fiddled with those settings from the drop-down menu.

She poked her head into the office just as the label maker whirred to life. It had been broken for nearly a month and I had just fixed it in a few minutes.

"I'm so grateful," she said as she gazed at me almost in adoration. "What can I do? Let me take you out for your favourite dish. Pumpkin cake."

"Can we go to the JiaJiang noodle house?" This was a restaurant I had been to before, just around the corner from her fortune cookie shop, and down the street – a stone's throw from the school.

"They have the best pumpkin cake. I knew you wouldn't say no." She giggled like she had beaten me, knowing I couldn't resist.

The noodle house faced a small road, free from cars, which sloped up. It sat a good three to six metres above the sidewalk, with large plate-glass windows looking over the road. We had to walk up the steep staircase to its door.

The servers were all boys and young men, not yet of age, wearing black smocks embroidered with gold, a passable likeness of imperial guard uniforms. They stood with their hands behind their backs, yelling their greetings as we came in. Wherever we turned, they shouted welcoming words, as if they were soldiers in the presence of officers.

Seated by the window in the peaceful restaurant, overlooking the old, brick road outside, I felt like I was back in ancient China, a messenger for the emperor. The specialty here was a soupless noodle covered with toppings, accompanied by a bowl of brown bean sauce.

"What are you planning to do after this?" the young accountant asked.

"I don't know, maybe go home and study. I have a lot of pages to read tonight."

"No, I mean, after the term is over."

"Oh, well, I haven't thought that far."

"I was thinking, it's almost Spring Festival. Do you have any plans? Want to come with me when I go home to visit my village?"

I knew it wasn't a romantic gesture. If she'd regarded me as her boyfriend, she wouldn't have invited me – unless she was sure I was going to marry her. So she considered me a friend, her best friend. How many people treated me that sincerely? I was so moved and also heartbroken by her innocence and naïveté, I didn't know how to answer.

The server came and took our orders. "Please give us a double serving of pumpkin cake as well," I added.

"Look at you, it's been a year, and just look at how you speak now," the accountant said, staring at me. She puffed me up a bit more, but it was the way her eyes gleamed when she looked at me that made me happy.

The cakes came and of course they were delicious. As we were eating, halfway through, she excused herself to use the bathroom. It was outside the restaurant, just by the entrance door. While she was gone, I got up and went to the bar, where the cashier was. She would be upset, but I paid for the meal. She wouldn't find out until we were about to leave, anyway.

She came back and continued to eat. "So what do you think? Want to come to my village?"

I hadn't yet been outside of the big city. I didn't know the village, the countryside, the country the way she knew it.

She sensed my hesitation. "You'll see a lot. It's nothing like this place. I'm sure you'll like it."

"I have to think about it," I said. I didn't tell her I was scared of what I would discover, about my people and about myself. "Where's the bathroom?"

"It's just out the front door, to the right. Go through the old brick wall there."

Outside, looking up, I could see that the sky, usually grey and thick with smog, had split open into a transcendent blue. To my left was the steep staircase going back down to the street. To the right was a crumbling wall with an opening in it.

I found a little square courtyard, enclosed by brick on every side. Near the far wall was a stone hut with a mud ditch in the ground. I went into the hut, and after finishing, came out.

For a moment, I stood, looking up at the sky. Behind the stone outhouse, I noticed, was a hole in the brick wall large enough to step through. Curious, I stuck my head through to the other side.

It was an unexpected sight. For miles around, I saw grass, forest, trees and flowers blooming. It was so eerily quiet, I looked for groundskeepers, staff, children, anyone at all. I only felt the wind against my face.

3.
The Delivery Boy

DELIVERY BOY — HE WASN'T KNOWN BY THIS NAME UNTIL later — was from the southern part of China, in the Canton region near the South China Sea. He travelled north to the capital not because he wanted to, but because it seemed like that was what everyone was doing. And he did not know what else to do.

"There's lots of money to be made," people said. "Jobs just waiting for strong country hands."

What Delivery Boy wanted was to stay in his hometown and start his own little business. He wanted to be a chef. He was good at making a specialty dish, a kind of soup called bohw tangh that only southerners ate. It was made in large stone vase-shaped bowls, and it was delicious. Nobody could make a more delicious bohw tangh than Delivery Boy.

As a child, he had learned the recipe from his grandmother. Bohw tangh could be made with any ingredients, or "wan wu jie kebao," as long as there was lots of meat. But her recipe, made of winter melon, seaweed, lean pork, sun-dried orange peel and flavoured with a secret pickled sauce, was especially tasty. Before she died, she had given him an exquisitely made, miniature bohw tangh bowl. He had no other possessions of value and treasured this fine stone bowl more than anything else. Beside her deathbed, holding the bowl, he had promised her that he would become a famous chef, known throughout the country.

He did not know how to fulfill this promise, however. "You don't have any money," everybody said. "You're too young to start a restaurant. Work a little bit, save up something. Then you'll be able to start your own catering company. Just like you want."

It seemed like that was what everybody was doing. Every young person from the countryside had to go to the city. Every young person had to work a bad job. At least for a little while. That was part of growing up. Part of what it meant to be a modern-day Chinese youth. Young people who didn't see the glamour of the big city but spent their whole lives in the villages, well, they were really tooh. They were "backward potatoes." Country hicks.

In the city, Delivery Boy didn't pay much attention to the wide avenues, cement pillars and herds of people. The whole ugly place was paved over, with monstrous glass castles bursting up. The air was thick with smog. For the first month, he didn't see the sky. Besides that, he discovered that everything was more expensive – food, or a place to sleep. He kept counting the money in his pocket. He feared that somehow it would disappear on its own.

Of the billboards, of the good-looking faces painted on them, he didn't think much. He walked on the sidewalk and over fields of tar. Across bridges that towered in the sky. He passed crowds of aging, tired office workers and crowds of glamorous young people with shopping bags, talking on cellphones. They seemed to clump together in groups. Delivery Boy looked twice, envious of the rich young men.

But Delivery Boy belonged nowhere. Who would ever hire him for an office job? He spoke with a strange southern accent. In the big city that was all it took for people to look down on you. A real company wanted young, fresh-faced Chinese who spoke English with American or British accents. Or at least a pure, clear

Putonghua, a spoken Chinese that was very precise and pleasing to listen to. He wasn't fresh-faced. He had a thick neck, shaved head, a square jaw. He had strong brown hands and muscular legs. He was sure he would never fit into a business suit with his wide body. He didn't have the skills needed to work in an office, and nobody wanted him there either.

That didn't mean, however, that there weren't jobs to be had. Young men like him had no education. But they were physically strong.

Out on the street he saw construction workers. They slept by the dozens on dusty bedrolls. Right out on the sidewalk. They lay all over the place at night, wherever there was an empty spot. During the day they were up and working. For half an hour at noon, they sat on the curb, eating their lunches.

But that was a difficult life. You didn't take a job like that unless you were hard up. Delivery Boy knew how little they were paid. He looked at the faces of the men who did those jobs. Hard, wind-bitten, wrinkled faces. All sunburnt until they were a deep reddish sort of brown. When it got cold out, they kept working. The only moisture in their faces was in the eyes, wet with tears they may not have even felt. The youngest were in their thirties. Some were sixty or nearing seventy. To be seventy and have to work like that – digging ditches, climbing up girders, carrying concrete blocks on a bent back – that was a bitter lot.

Then he saw mailmen. Groups of young male runners who knelt on the side of the street. They sorted out mountains of mail and packages. Delivery men of all types, riding trike-carts around, carting stuff back and forth. The business of the city depended on these bodies, who were invisible to most people.

Or he could work as a busboy somewhere. Or for a grocery store or whatever. He could do a hundred different odd jobs that required strong labour. He looked at the windows of the restaurants and shops. Many of them posted Help Wanted signs.

At first, he wanted to work in a restaurant. But the restaurants only hired locals, people whom they assumed would be stable and reliable. They didn't want to waste time training a stranger like him; he could leave the city without warning. Besides that, his heavy accent and the fast-paced environment of the restaurant didn't mix well. The kitchen staff would have no patience with trying to understand him, and the cooks all spoke the Beijing dialect anyway. So he looked for a job elsewhere.

This bakery shop was a classy place, all streamlined, following the protocols of 'Western'-style businesses. The store was part of a franchise. There were three of them in the city so far. They all followed the same set of instructions, the same recipes. They all got their equipment from the same place.

Delivery Boy liked the business from the start. The shopfront was clean. There was a thick window, with a bright orange sign over top. The store's name shone in neon yellow. The location wasn't bad either, in a strip plaza that curved around a corner. There was a modest supermarket, some retail outlets for the latest fashions. There was a phone store that was not at all rundown.

From the street, passersby could see the bakers mixing ingredients and baking cakes. At the back of the store, customers sat by another glass room where other bakers made pastries.

Delivery Boy's nostrils quivered. The brightly lit store had a wonderful, sweet smell of fresh baked goods.

When Delivery Boy walked in, he saw five pretty young girls wiping down the tables and counters. They opened the door for him, saying, "Huanying guang lin," in a cheery voice. Others were helping customers pick the tastiest treats. An older woman entered, draped in fur and shiny necklaces, escorted by her young daughter. Another customer was a well-dressed young man. After parking his fancy car, the young man came inside with his beautiful female companion.

So, Delivery Boy was taken on as, well, a delivery boy, because that was what he was best fit for. He pedalled a tricycle-cart to pick up crates of eggs from the market, or tubs of ingredients for the bakers. When he was done that, in the morning, he delivered cakes – if there were cakes to be delivered. If there weren't, he would take his cart and bike over to the offices in the surrounding area, armed with store brochures that pictured the smooth, expensive-looking cakes. Delivery Boy would try to sell them, working on commission.

The first month, he worked twenty-nine days, and took two off. That's to say, he worked through weekends. He had not been paid anything yet. At the end of the second month, he was paid his first month's earnings, based on a meagre monthly salary and a sales bonus. If the employee did something wrong, the employee would forfeit this money. Of course, anybody could be sacked at any time.

In order to maximize the work ethic and abilities of the employees, the owner forced them to live together in a little dormitory. It was free accommodation. But whenever an employee complained about the low salary, the owner would say, "You have a place to live and food to eat, don't forget that." Whenever the threat of being fired was not enough to make the employees compliant, the threat of being kicked out with nowhere to live did the trick. The owner was always willing to show his power. "You're fired. Move your bags out this evening, or else we'll confiscate them." Delivery Boy would have to lug all his bags and blankets and personal belongings out into the street. If it was wintertime, he would be at a complete loss.

However, Delivery Boy did not think about this. He thought it was a good set-up, not having to worry about a place to live. Even though he was somewhat of a loner, being around his coworkers, having a network and a routine, comforted him. He didn't feel so hopeless anymore.

The employee dormitory was part of an underground residence, known as a dixiashi, found across the street, at the back of an apartment complex. The entryway was a little shack with a stairwell that angled down.

The entrance served as the only exit. True, there was an emergency exit. But for the last decade it had been locked from the outside with half a dozen rusty bicycle locks.

"How many people live down here?" Delivery Boy asked his neighbour. There were about a hundred people. All living together, in that underground place, with that one tiny exit. Delivery Boy walked through the winding, turning corridors, which split, turned around on themselves, joined back up, split and split.

Soon Delivery Boy forgot how many turns he had made. He passed by many tiny, dark rooms housing strange people. One room had a huge mattress that covered the entire floor. A dozen dirty, tired men in work clothes lay sleeping there together without blankets.

There was a common bathroom, shared by the residents. It was an odd set-up. A miniature door, raised above the floor. A soggy wood ramp led up to it, with a soiled rubber mat. Inside the low-ceilinged bathroom, Delivery Boy had to crouch.

Here there was no squeamishness about the sexes, not like in universities where the girls and boys were kept strictly apart. Where, if a male student tried to enter the female dorm, the old aunty guarding the door would start yelling and snapping her fingers. Here, nobody cared what time you came or went. There was no curfew. These were young, uneducated women, teenagers from the villages whose families had no use for them. They came to the city to live in these places. They used these bathrooms, wearing only their pyjamas and slippers, soaping their armpits. They washed their faces at mouldy, slime-covered troughs with hard, bitter water. Behind them, strange men brushed past, sometimes groping and fondling them.

In the recesses of the labyrinth, hidden away in the farthest corner, was a crooked unlit stairwell, so narrow one had to slide sideways up between the walls. This stairwell led into the 'attic,' where the bakery workers lived.

This 'attic' was an apartment made up of dimly lit, stuffy rooms. Sometimes the employees would eat their meals here. They cooked over little hot plates. The odour would linger for days, mixing with smells of damp socks, blankets, dirty bodies. There were piles of crumbs, discarded food, fishbones on the concrete floor. Often there were arguments over the mess.

"Stop throwing your dirty food on the ground," shouted a woman, one of the employees. The young man she was yelling at jumped up from his bunk and kicked the pile of leftovers, scattering food scraps, chicken bones, chewed-up greens and half-digested rice under the bunks.

"Stop, don't do that anymore. I'm sick of living with you people!"

"What are you going to do about it? If you like, I can put the garbage on your bed!"

She burst into sobs, and ran out the door, rubbing her eyes. The other employees, out of uniform, sat on their beds, staring off. One of them, lying on an upper bunk, turned to face the wall.

All the men smoked in their rooms, even at night. Four men lived in one room, and three in another, with a flickering, fuzzy television always blaring. Delivery Boy smoked just as much as the others, in the end.

But it was a fine life, in a way. The employees were all young. Relationships and romances formed between them. Some of the young shopgirls were free-spirited village girls who had nowhere else to go, who were made mature beyond their age by circumstances, who had become independent, far away from parents who might have watched over them.

For eight months, Delivery Boy worked like this. When nobody was around, he would go to his bunk and uncover that most precious object: his vase-shaped bowl. He kept it carefully packed in a simple cardboard box with foam. It wasn't that life was unhappy. He just didn't want to forget the idea that he was destined for something else. He didn't want to forget the promise that he had made to his grandmother.

One day he borrowed a hot plate from a co-worker, the assistant baker, and tried making his bohw tangh. But he didn't have the right equipment. He didn't have all the ingredients he needed, and he couldn't spare the time or money to buy them.

"What's that you're making?" asked the assistant baker.

"It's a recipe from my hometown."

"Sure smells good."

Delivery Boy took out his stone bowl and showed the assistant baker. Delivery Boy felt happier, stood straighter, now that someone had seen his fine possession.

"You come from a good family, don't you?"

He nodded. "This belonged to my grandmother."

When the soup was ready, Delivery Boy poured a serving for the assistant baker and one for himself.

The assistant baker held a spoonful up to his nose and breathed in, relishing the aroma. He sipped quietly. "Very flavourful. I don't think I've ever had soup like this."

"No." Delivery Boy shook his head. "It should be better. I don't have what I need."

Delivery Boy listened more than he talked. When he wanted to do something, it was always by himself. Once, on a day off, he went to a hot pot restaurant. He liked hot pot and had saved up to treat himself to a good meal. But he had nobody to go with. Everyone knew that hot pot was a communal meal, meant to be enjoyed in a group. He thought about asking the assistant baker, but the baker was working that day. So Delivery Boy sat in the shop alone with the boiling soup pot in front of him. The servers came with slices of meats and vegetables. Although he enjoyed the smells, he could feel the eyeballs of the other patrons looking at him. Nobody ever ate hot pot alone. It was the loneliest thing a person could do.

Despite the hardships, time passed quickly. He got used to living with the others. Going to work for such long hours and doing nothing else seemed normal, since it became entirely one's life, and that satisfied the owner and managers.

He did not particularly enjoy the job. But when people asked him, he would brag about it, saying that he was a good salesman. He embellished stories about his commissions and how he had sold cakes to such and such a group of wealthy men.

It wasn't especially hard work. But it was time-consuming, and he wasn't paid very well for his trouble. Every time he met someone new, he would ask what they did, and how much money they were paid. Everyone seemed to be making more money than he was. He knew that the office workers were making two or three thousand a month. Those were the unskilled office workers. In the employment newspapers there were advertisements that showed skilled jobs, like technicians, or computer programmers, making four or five thousand. Then there were businessmen, and the Chinese who worked with foreigners from America and Europe. All making ten thousand. Here he was breaking his back for three hundred. Three hundred, for a month of his life. That was enough to buy just two of the bakery's cakes.

To make matters worse, he was feeling tired, physically sick, from the poor nutrition. Their diet consisted of rice and bean sprouts, and other vegetables. There was no protein. Even tofu would have helped. He made so little, it seemed that the bakery should at least give him good food to eat. But it didn't. He was only fed two paltry meals for lunch and dinner. Breakfast wasn't paid for by the bakery, a fact that Delivery Boy had protested more than once to the manager.

One morning, waking up hungry and tired, Delivery Boy wanted to have breakfast. He could have stopped to buy a little hot egg wrap or a bowl of plain congee – that would have satisfied his stomach. But, feeling mistreated by his employer, he took two eggs from the bakery. He boiled the eggs and ate them plain. In fact, a bowl of congee or a steamed bun would have tasted much better. It would only have cost a single kuai, just a dollar. But he deliberately, it appeared, wanted to steal from the bakery.

The next week, one evening, the store manager came in. He had seen a videotape. There were surveillance cameras in the store. Delivery Boy had been caught on tape.

"You're fired, what more is there to say?" said the manager. "Pack your things and get out of here."

"Why? What did I do?"

"The video recording of you stealing the eggs, we've all seen it."

"So what, two eggs? You're firing me over two stolen eggs?"

"Of course, who can trust you? Get the hell out of here before we call the police."

"I'll gladly go, but I want my salary first."

"You still have enough balls to ask for your salary? Do you want to go to prison too?"

"Two eggs for two months' wages. Your abacus is too clever!"

"What's your decision? You want to leave or do you want to go to jail?"

"You think I'm stupid? Two eggs, how long does a person stay in prison for two eggs? Go on, figure out how much you owe me. You can subtract the cost of the two eggs!"

Six hundred yuan was a lot of money, money that he needed to start his dream. In front of all the staring customers and his fellow employees, Delivery Boy trembled. The assistant baker, the one person who had tasted his bohw tangh, watched through the window that separated the sales floor from the kitchen.

"Enough, I don't want to talk anymore." The manager reached into a duffle bag and took out a cardboard box. "Look for yourself, if you keep yelling and damaging my store's reputation, I'll damage your property too, fair is fair."

Delivery Boy looked. His grandmother's bowl.

"You went through my things?"

"Of course, you're living in my place, I pay the rent. Whenever I want to go in, I'll go in. I know how much this object means to you. Either I call the police now, or you take your worthless bowl and get lost."

The manager walked over and opened the door. He placed the bowl on the ground outside.

"All right, get out of here, I don't want to see you again." The manager waved his hand, not bothering to look at Delivery Boy, waving as though he were shooing away a dog.

Outside, a public bus pulled up. Delivery Boy didn't look back at the shop. He got onto the bus, cradling his bowl in his arms.

"Where's your fare?" The bus driver tapped the collection box. Delivery Boy reached into his empty pocket. He could feel the bus driver staring at him. He shook his head and stared at the floor.

"Got nothing?" The driver sighed. "Okay, forget it, go have a seat."

He staggered as the bus lurched forward. At the back row, he sat down and looked out the window, his eyes searching the dusty streets.

4.
The Drunkard

ONE

BEFORE THE WEDDING WAS TO TAKE PLACE, THE BRIDE wanted to have an engagement photo shoot done, a prerequisite that had become popular among young couples. This was easy enough, as she had a friend who recommended a nearby studio. They went that very day and picked the cheapest package.

The package included four outfits to wear for the shoot. Like cheap clothes on Taobao, the outfits looked better than they were worth, the material thin and scratchy. Some garments were Victorian-era fashions, gowns with narrow, pointed waists and bell-shaped skirts, with layers of petticoats. Some were classic or traditional Chinese qipaos. The package included a full day with the photographer and a makeup artist at a special complex for wedding photo shoots.

The enormous complex, once a failed shopping mall, had hundreds of rooms: 267, exactly. Each room had a different design, like a movie set. So many rooms that no one brochure featured them all. First the photographer took them to an adjacent outdoor park.

"Let's do the sunflowers first," the bride said.

There was a dense field of sunflowers. They went into the flowers, carefully stepping in the wild weeds. Insects buzzed around their heads and the sun streamed down. It was uncomfortable and hot, but the bride was thrilled by the delicate flowers. "Hold me up," she said to the groom.

The groom tried lifting her. He bent awkwardly, stooped some more and put his arms around her knees.

"Not like that. Like in the movies."

"I can't, my back hurts," the groom said.

"You're impossible. Just try it, for a second. We need a good picture."

He tried once more, hefting her up. The photographer took a photo, catching the image of her in the air, her hair glistening in an elaborate bun, her knees bent back, her feet up behind her. She loved the feeling of having her chin tilted back, her face to the sun.

How beautiful I'm going to look in these photos, she thought.

"Should we do the big sign next?" asked the groom. There was a big three-dimensional sign on a grassy hill near them that featured an English word: *LOVE*.

"No, that's dumb. Let's do the hot-air balloon."

It was a fake hot-air balloon made of plaster or hard plastic. It was painted red and white, and although the paint was peeling off and the metal mesh could be seen underneath, it still made for a striking image.

"Spread your hands out," the photographer said. "Look like you're having fun."

"Like this?" She waved her hands.

"Look like you're falling off, out of the basket."

She laughed and laughed. She had never done a photo shoot like this. She felt like a movie star.

* * *

Once these photos were taken, they went into the mall. They chose half a dozen rooms to pose in for photos. There was the Snow Palace room, which looked like a dreamy frozen icicle cave with a snow-covered old ship. The ship's masts towered above them. The Classic European room with European paintings on the walls, and velvet couches surrounded by flowers and patio doors, Victorian trim tables, candlesticks and a piano. There was the Plum Tree room and castle, and, of course, the Traditional Chinese red room, complete with cherry blossom trees.

In each room the makeup artist redid the young bride's hair and face. She was like a celebrity, with her flashy looks. She wanted to enjoy it, because soon she would be a housewife and few people would pay attention to her anymore.

One shoot was playful, in a quiet, out-of-the-way room over-decorated like the others. Here, the photographer took a few saucy photos where the bride wore only underwear like a brassiere and panties. *The youth are so outrageous these days, they are positively shameless*, she thought. She was embarrassed, but everyone was doing it.

"Don't be shy," said the photographer, "you look good. Spread your arms and legs more, look confident."

The young bride threw her head back, letting her long hair fall against her back. She pouted her lips, even stuck out her tongue and batted her eyelashes. In another photo, she placed her hands on her hips and looked as tough and as sensual as she dared. It was almost scandalous how good she was at it. When that shot was done, she cupped her own two breasts, hidden behind a heavily padded bra, and squeezed them together while sticking her entire naked left leg out. With the high heels on, she was tall and glamorous. She put her foot on a stool and bent forward, jutting out her bottom toward the camera.

As she tried these poses, each one more provocative, her back began to break out into a cold sweat. When the photographer urged her on, her armpits grew clammy. Her stomach churned and she swallowed to keep from vomiting. This wasn't fun anymore, not at all. The photographer had a loud voice and was singing a little as he spoke, when he thought she couldn't hear him.

"Smile a bit more, look happier!"

"I don't know how, I'm trying."

"Think about if you won five hundred thousand RMB in the lottery. You have to pick up the prize tomorrow! What are you going to spend your money on?"

"A Louis Vuitton bag."

"Hey, that's perfect! Keep smiling. Dance too, if you want."

"I'd want a Chanel perfume set. And plenty of other stuff."

The photographer started whistling an upbeat tune. However, as soon as he stopped encouraging her, she had trouble keeping up her fake smile. He was a handsome guy, there was nothing creepy about him at all. He spoke with the accent of her hometown village, which should have put her at ease, but instead had the opposite effect. He sounded like so many men she had known, or like one in particular she couldn't forget.

"Tell your woman to loosen up," he said to the husband-to-be. "Maybe give her a hug. Or a poke."

TWO

The wedding date came quickly. The main road was paved, with trees lining the shoulders. Beyond that were more trees, fields, farms, dense clusters of brick huts and endless networks of dirt paths.

The family's house was deep inside the village, and like the others, had a grand front gate facing a small single-lane dirt road. Inside the gate was the courtyard, and set back was the main house with one living room and attached bedroom on the ground floor. On the second floor were three more small bedrooms.

The only other rooms on the property were brick sheds attached to the sides of the front gate. The kitchen was on the left, a brick shack with a rooftop terrace where the family kept a tiny chicken coop with seven chickens, which were never let out. Under the staircase was the family dog, which had been chained for the last decade. The dog was crippled because as a pup it had been bitten by a large dog. Everyone was ashamed of this face-losing fact.

Opposite the kitchen was a storage closet and a shower room. The bathroom was a hole in the mud outside the gate, by the dusty public road.

So this was the home where the young bride had grown up, when she was not being fobbed off on one relative or another. She liked being home, in her old bedroom, the one in the middle of the hall. There was a dresser made of a fabric tarp stretched across plastic rods, a contraption the young wife had bought from Taobao years ago. This dresser was still there, after all this time.

Her father had fixed up the house in advance of the wedding. He had also organized friends to prepare food and pitch tents on the road for guests. It was a big deal, a wedding. The mother of the bride was there to meet her as well, as she arrived.

The grandfather and grandmother were present too, grandfather sitting with one leg crossed over the other, a cigarette in his mouth. Grandmother was stooped, a frail woman looking older than her age, with her grey hair in a ponytail.

The father showed off the recent renovations, the new paint upstairs, the new door, the ceiling in the living room. He had hired a company specializing in remodelling people's ceilings. The company's ads could be found on the hydro poles all along the streets for miles around. Every home in the village had the same design with a main hall ceiling, so it was good business. There were five types of ceiling lights to choose from, all fancy and modern with disco-style coloured lights.

"So nice, it must have been expensive," the young wife said, pointing at the ceiling. The father nodded, everyone nodded.

A handful of other villagers had come to greet her, including a red-faced man in his twenties, whose face looked quite childish. This man stood behind the crowd, somewhat apart. The young bride remembered him from her youth. He was in school, a few years older than her. He was the first boy she had spent time with alone, it came back to her.

"You, me," the red-faced man – then a boy – had said. "You, me." The words had been accompanied by giggling. Not the innocent kind.

THREE

"You've been away too long," said the grandmother. "Next time don't stay away for so long."

The bride knew she should visit more. She had told herself that she didn't like that undeveloped part of the country. There was no plumbing, none of the comforts of urban life. Like all young people, she had moved to a city, the nearest city with flushing toilets.

She was embarrassed by her village. The poor facilities, the mud bathroom, the mosquitoes. Everywhere people were blowing smoke. Grandmothers cradling babies had cigarettes between their lips. Everyone was happy and enjoying themselves far away from the worries of the modern world, but all the bride could see was the raw sewage on the side of the road, the garbage piled in the rocky field behind the houses.

Even so, she was happy to see her grandmother and grandfather. Especially her grandmother who took care of her when she was a child. Of all her relatives, the grandmother was the most relieved that the young bride had found someone to marry.

"Now be quick about having a baby boy," the grandmother said.

The toothless smile on her grandmother's face pleased the young bride. If she was marrying someone from a different province and had to move far away, the grandmother would be upset. Instead of sitting in the corner angrily weeping and giving everyone the silent treatment, now the grandmother was clapping her hands and grinning. It was perfect, a continuation of harmonious society.

On the first day of the wedding, there was not much for either the bride or groom to do. It was all taken care of by the father's village friends. People came and ate on the dirt road outside the gate, under tents. On both sides of the road were weeds, overgrown trees, bushes.

For food, there was a stretch wheelbarrow contraption, a mobile cooking station with four big woks, a long hollow body underneath full of wood logs and ash. A team of cooks worked all week preparing vast amounts of food.

In the storage room by the kitchen was a wood bunk. On the bunk, and over the floor, the cooks kept all the dishes that had been made for the day. Dozens of whole chickens were simmered together in the mobile cooking wagon, as well as thick stews and spicy soups and every kind of local delicacy that people liked, such as super spicy Mao Dou bean salad and secret smoked anchovies. The head cook wore a straw hat like a cowboy and no shirt, and loose grey work shorts.

Since there was little for the groom and bride to do, they were bored. In the late afternoon, the groom had an idea.

"Let's take the family dog for a walk." The bride thought hard but could not remember ever having taken the dog for a walk.

"But it's lame. Why take it out and let people see our family's dark secret?"

"We'll take him just for a short walk." Why not? The worst that could happen was that the neighbours would see, gossip and laugh at them behind their backs until the bride's family lost all dignity.

"What's the dog's name?" the groom asked.

"Why would it have a name? It's not a pet, it's here to guard the property."

The dog was so dirty, its grey coat was putrid. Flies buzzed all around it. Nobody wanted to go near that thing. But that did not deter the idealistic groom. Down the street they walked, the three of them – the bride, the groom and the dog on a leash. The dog walked well enough, albeit with a limp.

Just as the bride had worried, the elderly neighbours a few doors down were sitting on a stoop in front of a garage. They called boorishly as the two walked by with the dog.

"Don't you have any shame? What fools," said the old man. The bride pretended not to hear, but her face got red. She didn't want to blame the groom's stupid suggestion. All she could do was glare menacingly at the neighbours who whispered and snickered to each other.

"What's the matter with your household?" shouted another old man. One of the women spat on the ground in disgust at the lame dog. It was just the charming rural etiquette. The bride had no one to blame but herself.

By the time they reached the forest path along the river, the dog could walk no farther. This was probably due to its bad leg and lack of exercise. It lay down in the dirt and however much the couple pulled the leash, the dog refused to budge.

"Pick him up," said the groom. The unwelcome job was left to the bride, the woman.

"I can't," she said, after trying, "it's too dirty."

The groom tried to drag it, but again it just lay in the dirt. He tried to lift the dog up and carry it. But even he was surprised by the smell and was forced to put it back down. So there they were, the three of them – groom, bride and dirty dog – stuck in the forest.

After a while, with some persistent tugging, the dog got on its three good legs and hopped along. In time they came to some villagers picking beans from a pile of leafy branches. To one side children played in the dirt. One of the children had a little toy wagon.

"Little boy," said the bride, "can we borrow your wagon?" The boy nodded. The young wife picked up the dog and lowered it into the toy.

Along the way home, the sun set. Passing by the driveway of an abandoned lot, a dozen aunties danced with a boom box blaring, as they did every evening. Watching them was a drunk man holding a fire-red jug. In the daytime, he stood half-naked, pouring alcohol from this gasoline tank over his face, singing and yelling incoherently.

"He's from our village," the young wife whispered. "He's got a bad brain."

Without looking at the drunk, the young wife could remember the smell, the feelings, the hot hands on her body. She turned away then and looked down at the dog, and swore she could see sadness in its round brown eyes.

FOUR

Villagers erected air-filled arches up and down the road. These had red banners proclaiming the marriage union between the bride and the groom. Different relatives sponsored each of these arches, which listed their names along with well wishes.

On the night before the wedding, the groom stayed in the town hotel. It was a local custom. In the morning, his friends picked him up at the hotel in rented cars. They drove him over to where the bride was, in the village, in the parents' house.

The time had come. The young bride was sitting on the bed, surrounded by relatives, aunts and grandmother. Numerous children scampered about. The bride went to the window and looked outside. She could hear the firecrackers popping everywhere. The man of the hour was approaching.

Every few metres the cars stopped and someone got out to light the firecrackers. Clouds of smoke obscured the road. The band was clanging their instruments loudly and the horn was wailing. Already the bride's face was streaked with tears.

The groom had arrived. From the window she saw him throwing candies into the crowd. The red umbrella she had given him was in his hand. She could hear his footsteps coming up to the second floor. She saw the crowd part for him.

His head poked through the door. There was hardly any space in the room. Relatives stood in every corner, packed against the walls. The bride was sitting on the bed, her red slippers and red socks to one side.

"You l-look beautiful."

"Thank you." She wiped tears from her eyes. She held her hand out, and he knelt down and put a wedding ring on her finger. It wasn't a real ring, just a cheap plastic ring. But that didn't matter.

The bride presented her bare foot. She watched as the groom gently fitted the red slipper and sock.

Together they went down into the courtyard where they posed for group photos. "Let's kowtow to my nai nai, okay?" the bride said.

The new couple got down on their knees and grovelled in the courtyard, in front of grandmother and all the onlookers. The live band squalled over the amplifier. One of the neighbours complained and called the police because of all the loud noise. The bride and groom wanted to get the ceremony over with before it got interrupted; otherwise that would be bad luck.

The bride was looking out for the police. But when she scanned the crowd, she saw a familiar face, reddened, childish, standing near the house gate, squeezed between the crowds of onlookers.

She got up on her feet and pulled her new husband. As they made their way out of the courtyard, she could hear her family's dog barking from where it was, locked under the stairwell, out of sight of their guests.

She clutched her new husband's arm tighter. As they came to the car, the spectators around them tossed confetti. Amid the excitement, the bride felt a flick of wetness on her face. She reached up to clean her cheek. It was a gob of yellowish-white, sticky substance. In the confusion, she touched her finger to her tongue, and the pungent taste of semen made her gag.

FIVE

After leaving the wedding, the bride and groom met their friends at a restaurant by the only crossroad of the nearest town. On the sixth and top floor of the tallest building, they had a specially reserved room. Here they could eat and be merry in private.

The new couple took photos and went around the table, thanking everyone for coming. In turn the friends offered red pockets fat with lucky money. The couple raised their glasses with their friends.

"You two have to drink with each other, you can't just clink glasses with us," the friends shouted.

"Jiao bei jiu!"

The waiters served food and brought out more white wine, beer and Western-brand soda bottles, big two-litre bottles. There were many courses and dishes. Although the food wasn't that great, at least they were celebrating.

The most important thing was eating the longevity noodles. Everyone at the table watched the groom and bride pick up the noodles with chopsticks. The couple took turns feeding each other.

Toward the end of the meal, the bride felt bloated and excused herself.

"Where's the bathroom?" she asked the waitress.

"Follow the hallway all the way down, at the end."

She went by herself, following the corridor. The walls and floors seemed to get dirtier, and already there was a bad smell.

Finally she found a sign on a door, tucked away in a corner. As she opened the door, however, she stumbled back.

The red-faced man was hiding inside. He grabbed at her chest, clutching her to him. He pulled her hair, craning her neck back painfully.

"I love you," he whispered. He dragged his red tongue across her face.

The young bride had felt this before. When she was twelve, he had found her picking weeds in an abandoned field, weeds that she'd pretended were pretty flowers. He had put his hands on her then, just like this. The only difference was, back then, she didn't know what was going to happen.

As he touched her, she closed her eyes and thought back to her wedding. She remembered how they had left the village, her parents, her grandmother.

The procession had been slow. She could see all the villagers walking in front of the car, setting off fireworks. Among them the brass band played an ancient Xuzhou marriage marching song. The bride could hear it, the beautiful song that she loved, that had brought her to tears.

5.
The Girl from Dongguan

FOR THE LAST FEW YEARS, YOU TRIED TO MAKE A LIFE IN Dongguan, in a tiny city located in the south of China, near Hong Kong.

It had a public hospital, only one movie theatre and supermarket, a two-floor unlit computer mall across the street, one downtown road and town square, a two-room city library, a Japanese restaurant, a clothing mall, phone street and eating street. Right in the middle was a local tourist attraction, a manmade rectangular pond full of dead lilies and mosquitoes. Opposite this was a five-star hotel resort with an extravagant outdoor pool almost like a moat, with a waterfall, bridge and artificial beach. I remember it well, because we used to swim there together whenever we could.

Away from the downtown core was an international private high school. Around this area it was more industrial, with mom-and-pop shops selling copper and PVC pipes, furnishings and used appliances for the new buildings that were being erected.

In this industrial area were many small factories, one of which employed your parents. Later on, after you finished school, you came to work in its accounting department. This factory had about 150 employees. The owner was Taiwanese and came to visit the factory often.

For long-distance transportation, there was a bus depot across from the international school. The closest train station was an hour away in an adjacent town called Changping, where passengers could take a train directly into Hong Kong and which I myself took quite frequently.

We met one afternoon downtown, at a bus stop. There was a light summer breeze. You turned around and looked at me.

"Is this the right bus to take?" I asked.

"That depends on where you're going."

"I'm going to the international school."

"Yes, this is the right bus."

"Good, thanks. I'm new to the city," I said. This wasn't true since I had been there for a few months and knew which bus to take. But I wanted to talk to you.

You looked away, down the street, waiting for the bus, as if you had already forgotten me. But maybe you could feel me still staring at you, your long hair flowing down to the small of your back. Maybe you didn't want me to think you were easily intimidated and unassertive.

"Where do you work?" you asked.

I didn't tell you then that I was a foreigner. I only told you that I worked for the international private school, the only one in that city. It was a very expensive school whose campus was fortified like an island base, just twenty minutes' walk from the factory where you worked.

On the bus we talked the entire time. I can't remember what we said, but it was like a dream. Before getting off I asked for your phone number. You didn't hesitate; you gave it to me right away. I stood as the bus turned a corner, waving, and you sat there watching me, your face a mask as always.

I didn't know but later that night, you chatted online with a boy you had never met in real life. He had courted you for a long time, flattered you every day. He sent you gifts that I later saw: a 3-D puzzle-piece castle, a novelty-sized sand timer, snacks and other knickknacks purchased and mailed from Taobao.

A few days later, I went out to buy some water pipes.

I was in the process of making a desk for my tablet computer. I walked out along the road, off-campus, visiting the water pipe shops. There were dozens of them all down the street because construction was everywhere. The owners of these shops themselves made racks from water pipes. They put these on the wide driving lot that spanned the shop entrances to dry their laundry in the sun.

Eventually I bought what I needed. But the pipes were so heavy that I had to take the bus back. It was a coincidence, but I got on the bus and saw you sitting there, like a vision in a desert. You waved and I sat down beside you. You asked me what I was doing, why I was carrying so many pipes like a plumber.

The next evening I waited outside your factory gate. We walked up and down the dusty road, the only road in that area. We passed more industrial plots. The factories were small, and batches of young people wearing uniforms strolled up and down under the dim street lights.

At the end of the road was a small intersection with a narrow, rundown seven-storey building with bare concrete walls. The stairwell windows looking out onto the street had no glass. It was the tallest building around. On the ground floor was a convenience shop.

I was always drawn to women like you – subdued, serious and melancholy. You seldom laughed, but I loved it when you did. You had what I started to think of as an introspective longing, a regret that hung over you and tinged everything you said. It wasn't so much your words, it was more the way you stared at me with such quiet intensity whenever we spoke.

That week I came almost every night after work, to wait for you by your factory gate. You lived in the compound, in a room together with your parents. It was all heavily guarded, so I couldn't go inside. But when you came out, we would have a stroll together.

There wasn't a decent place to walk, what with all the factories and bad air. But still, we were together. The two of us came upon an open gate, which was part of a residential set of bieshu houses along a black body of water. Perhaps in five or ten years those houses would be occupied by people who did business here, Hong Kongers or others who came to work in Dongguan. But at the moment, during the time we knew each other, they were abandoned.

We stood on a desolate concrete platform, looking out onto the manmade pond. On the opposite shore was an expensive restaurant, the only one in this area, which was also always unlit and empty.

I didn't put my arm around you. If I did, you probably would have run off. You sat on the concrete rail and looked out into the darkness.

We spent a long time in silence. You told me about your online boyfriend. Maybe you thought that would keep me at a distance. Even though you only hinted at it, I guessed the truth.

"He doesn't count as your boyfriend if you've never met him," I said.

A row of a dozen houses, each identical, looked out onto the water. We walked by them. There was a guard who lounged in a guardhouse by the pier. We were not supposed to be there, but the guard said nothing. In all my years in China, that was the only guard who didn't mind keeping his mouth shut.

"Do you know any magic tricks, Danny?"

"No, not really," I said. "But I have a photographic memory."

"Really? Prove it."

I had never done my trick, and it was something that I had just been playing with the night before. "Look up a number on your phone, any number, with as many digits as you want," I said.

You found a number, pi, as I'd hoped you would. "Let me see it," I said, and looked at your phone, pretending to memorize it.

After I handed your phone back, I began to recite it, about three hundred digits. You stayed silent the whole time. Even with only the lamplight casting shadows everywhere, your eyes sparkled.

"How?" you asked, finally. It was a cheap trick, and I made it worse. Instead of answering, I violated your space. I leaned forward and kissed you on the forehead. It was wrong of me, I know and I'm sorry. You pulled back, but it was too late, I had kissed you already.

Perhaps you thought you had betrayed your online boyfriend. Even a kiss on the forehead was a kiss. Maybe you asked yourself that night if you had done something wrong.

"I-I-I have to go. Goodnight –"

"Wait," I said.

But you did not wait. You ran off without looking over your shoulder. You disappeared into the darkness.

We met a couple of nights later. This was the first proper date we had, when you declared that you were no longer communicating with your online boyfriend. We met at a popular chain noodle shop by the downtown square, outside the movie house and mall. It was an elegant and upscale traditional HuiMin restaurant.

The tables were large and heavy, with marble centres and wood frames. A clean, well-lit kitchen in the back was separated by a floating glass wall. The soup noodle chef and stir-fry chef were at an open hot plate cooking.

That was the first time I saw you in a brightly lit place and I had a long time to examine you over dinner. When you showed up with your long hair parted in pigtails, I swore that if things did not work out between us, I would leave the country forever and never come back.

I didn't know then that, three years later, you would get lymphoma and die, and that, afterward, I would leave the country as I had promised myself, but only when it was too late.

* * *

After that night, our first formal date, I got into the habit of buying you snacks and tasty things online, all shipped to your factory address. You didn't tell me to do it, it just seemed to be what was expected. Now I regret not having bought more things for you when I'd had the chance to do so.

Later, when I left the country, it was too late to change what my life had become, to mourn you as I should have.

The school campus where I worked had a front and back gate, which was protected like a military compound. The students were from wealthy families all over Dongguan. Whenever we tried to enter, it was always difficult. I applied for a pass card for you, but, because we were not related and not married, the school administration would not give it to me. We often stood outside the gate while the young guards called and waited for someone with more authority to allow you entry.

Like the other teachers, I lived in one of two buildings near the back gate looking over the soccer field. I was on the eighth floor and occupied a two-bedroom apartment. I had a private bathroom, kitchen, balcony and a spare bedroom. The apartment was standard for foreign teachers, but I felt guilty.

For fun we slept on the floor of the living room, on a big blanket. We didn't have intimate relations. I knew you wanted space and time. I had already violated you once by kissing your forehead.

When summer came, I moved off-campus to be with you. It was so hard getting you through the guard gates onto the school campus that living off-campus was better anyway.

I moved into the seven-storey building by the intersection, at the end of the street where your factory was.

The rooms were so old and dilapidated, it was like a bombed-out shelter. The metal front door of each unit had a deadbolt and padlock on the outside, and a deadbolt on the inside. In our unit on the sixth floor, the bathroom didn't even have a sink, just a tap coming out of the wall and a shower head dangling off a wire. I bought an electric hot water heater and had it installed. I also added a sink bowl under the faucet. We went without a fridge. I bought a little toaster oven, which I used to grill eggplants and other veggies.

After moving in, on the first day, we heard laughter in the stairwell. There was a noise against our door. When I tried to open the door, I found it was locked from the outside. "Hey," I shouted. "Open up." But there was only more laughter.

You pushed me aside and pounded on the door, shouting loudly. The outer deadbolt slid open and you went into the hall. I didn't follow you but I could hear you yelling at the group who had played the trick. I looked out and saw three young men, a bit older than you, standing sheepishly with their heads bowed while you berated them.

Later that week, you moved in with me. You told your parents that you had found your own place outside the factory.

I had saved up a little money. That summer I bought a membership card for the swimming pool downtown, behind the nice hotel by the rectangular lily pond.

We would go together almost every day. You loved that pool so much. There was an exercise room on one shore, behind glass, and we would use the ellipticals and treadmills before swimming. It took me days before I had fully mapped out the entire pool, which ran like a winding moat, branching out in a dozen directions, with trees and shrubs shrouding everything.

We took trips that summer. Once to Shenzhen, to the Window of the World. We went to all the replicas: the fake Eiffel Tower, the Louvre Pyramid, the windmills and tulips of the Netherlands, the Borobudur Temple, Angkor Wat, Mount Rushmore, the Statue of Liberty, the Colosseum, St. Peter's Basilica and the Leaning Tower of Pisa. We took so many photos – or I did, since you hated taking photos. Later on, we lost those photos. I left them on a portable drive, in a cardboard box, and you threw it out.

"What's the point of keeping photos?" you asked.

We had some copies on your computer too. "We should back them up," I said.

"Why?"

But your computer wouldn't turn on. You brought it over and we looked at it, but it was dead. "We should take the hard drive out, we can recover our photos."

"I don't want to," you said. "It's too much trouble."

I didn't understand why you didn't want those photos, or why photos didn't matter to you. Much later, when we were no longer together, I grieved for those photos of our time together. I thought I had copies elsewhere. I looked and looked, but I never found them again.

Once I got annoyed that you were using my tablet computer. After an argument, I went to the bathroom and when I came out, you were gone. I hadn't heard you leave the apartment. It was such a small place, I didn't know where you were hiding. You weren't in the bedroom, which didn't have any furniture except for my computer pipe table. You weren't in the kitchenette. You weren't in the little living area where we kept our bed. I looked under the covers and behind the door. I glanced out the window to the balcony, but you weren't there either.

I pushed the balcony door back. There you were, sitting with your buttocks and legs balancing lengthwise along the narrow concrete rail. Your back was leaning against the wall.

"What are you doing? Come on, get down, you're going to fall."

"Who cares if I do?"

I looked over the edge and got dizzy. A fall from that height was certain death. I slipped my arm in front of your stomach and around you, as close as I dared without touching you. I thought if you lost your balance, I'd be able to pull you back onto the balcony floor.

A month later, I went downtown. When I came back in the afternoon, I found you in our apartment, soaked in sweat.

"Check it out, it's your birthday present," you said, nodding to the bathroom. I stuck my head in and saw a compact-sized laundry machine.

"I carried it all the way upstairs. The delivery guy was a real jerk. He wouldn't help me."

It had a washer on the left, and a tiny dryer on the right. The dryer was a little plastic basket where we put in the wet clothes. We pressed a button and it would spin the clothes around, that's all the dryer did. I loved it so much.

The summer heat got worse and you couldn't stand it. "Can you buy a used air conditioner from the shop across the street?" you asked.

I was more than happy to, for you. I went downstairs. It was the building opposite the intersection, next to the restaurant that we often went to. In the morning the shop owner would retract the garage-style walls. There were piles of junked appliances. He sold me a massive air conditioner, it must have weighed three hundred pounds. His workers helped move it up to my little apartment and stuck it in the window over our balcony, so that if it fell out, it would only fall onto the balcony. Even set at maximum, only a little puff of cold air would putter out. But our electricity bill shot up by a thousand percent.

From our room on the seventh floor we overlooked the intersection. At night the long-distance trucks would blow through, blaring their horns, no matter what the colour of the light was. Now and then trucks came, loaded with cages full of squawking birds or groaning pigs and cattle. The stench would linger in our room long after.

After work, we would often meet at the nearby traffic light intersection. Everything here was always dusty. Old aunties sold lychees, melons, starfruit, countless varieties. They peeled and chopped sugar cane on the streets. On the main road was an EMS postal shop set back. By the intersection was an ugly triangular patch of grass. Here we met under a tree, away from the crowds, we lay in the grass, held each other for hours and kissed.

This is how I remember you.

Part Two: Courtship

6.
The Professor and the Student

HER DISSATISFACTION WITH LIFE, WITH SOCIETY, HER parents, the future, had more to do with her unhappy love life, or lack of one. That much she understood. That was the real reason for the void in her heart.

She had rejected all kinds of suitors, local men from average families. In all honesty, she had a secret that she often whispered to herself: she wanted to be a Taobao model. But she was too short, and, when she looked in the mirror at her rounded face, even she knew that she was only kidding herself. Now she was sitting in a large classroom of fellow students, in the front row, in her college English class. She had spent the whole hour staring at the English professor, John.

This John was handsome, it was undeniable. His physique wasn't great, but his face looked like a real American – Tom, Tim or Tony Something. She didn't know the names because handsome movie stars looked so similar. He had a certain charisma too, despite his beer gut and thinning hair. True, he was too old for her. Also, he was divorced, nearly forty or fifty. But she thought he had an adventurous spirit as she watched him bounce around the classroom, reciting words she could never retain. Whenever he asked the class a question, she ducked her head down shyly. Her heartbeat made her dizzy.

For a moment, sitting there, she weighed the benefits versus the drawbacks of pursuing an unorthodox relationship like this. When she graduated from college, she would be expected to marry. The question she knew her mother would ask was *Why not marry a homegrown boy? Why chase after one of those gangly foreigners?* To any reasonable person the answer was obvious. Yet she, with her chin in the palm of her hand, chewed on the question over and over.

For one, she argued to herself, a foreigner like John had so much to offer. She dreamed of his home in America: a ritzy neighbourhood with big brick houses, driveways and yards, sidewalks lined with maple trees. A fancy school nearby with a lineup of Audis and BMWs on the street outside; rich parents waiting to pick up their kids; white, blond and brown-haired teachers in every classroom; a pompous, over-the-top graduation ceremony with dignitaries speaking at a lectern. Opportunities of every kind, jobs and a future. She imagined herself flying home to China on annual visits for Spring Festival, drinking airplane champagne, basking in vanity.

Such mystery in those colourful eyes. And the way he spoke, such an authoritative manly voice. The stubble on his face, the hair on his hands – so masculine. What she wanted most was for him to take her to an art show. She knew nothing about art, but she wanted to try it, especially a kind of painting or performance art, involving, she had heard, lots of smelly frogs and naked women with hairy armpits. She imagined going to such an event with him, walking into a gallery or gazing at canvases outdoors on a cobblestone street. She would wear high heels so that she wouldn't appear too short for him. The envious stares she would get.

Not to mention all those benefits for her kids – *when* she had kids, that is: access to international education, some expensive private school with everything in English. Surely her children would be fluent in both English and Chinese. Perhaps, looking as cute as they would – with big round eyes, pale, ruddy-cheeked faces crowned with darkly coloured tufts of hair – they'd become media darlings in China and host their own television show.

Naturally she had taken Mao Zedong theory class, and she knew that America was evil. Well, if not evil, then at least morally corrupt and bad. Their leaders were corrupt and power hungry, their people had a history of troublemaking. But somehow that didn't translate into negative thoughts when she saw an American in person. Where did her teachers go wrong? The thought worried her for a moment, but she pushed it aside.

She wanted to see him after class and so she formed a plan: to ask him a question about grammar. Then, feigning innocence, she would follow up with a suggestion that they could discuss the point further over a cup of coffee. Since he was an American, he would be a coffee drinker, obviously. Even though she hated the strong, bitter beverage, she would happily endure sitting down over a drink so that she could gaze into his eyes. He would invite her to his teacher's apartment on the pretext of giving her some study materials. Perhaps she would sit on the couch to peruse the textbooks while he prepared some Western food in the kitchen. Some American hip hop music to set the mood, followed by a candlelit dinner and wine.

But her imagination was just that. Those things did not come to pass. In the hallway, after dismissal, she tittered with her school friend, Apple, who complained that she couldn't see the blackboard and more importantly, John's handsome face.

"You need glasses," she said to Apple, who pouted. Corrective lenses would obscure her pretty features.

Outside, the young student took Apple by the arm and walked across the campus yard, conscious of people's eyes following her. She was the prettier of the two, and knew that boys and young men often turned their heads to look wherever she went. If only John would look at her that way.

"Do you think John would really go for me?" she asked Apple.

"Maybe. But what will you get from a relationship with him?"

"He's a professor, he's got a good career. What girl wouldn't want to be married to him?"

"Sure. But you know how it is."

"What is?"

"He's not really a professor, is he? I mean, the job, he's kind of a gimmick, the goofy wai jiao, the school mascot."

"He's a foreigner, he can speak English. How is that a gimmick?"

"He's the only foreigner around. So of course he can get the job. He's the only guy who can speak English."

"That's not true, what about Dave? He's from Africa, he speaks English too."

"So what about him? Why not go after him? If John is a professor, so is Dave."

"Ha! John's handsome, Dave's not. Anyway, I can't understand Dave's English."

"I read somewhere that the media shapes our thinking so that we think white guys are more handsome than Black guys. It's pretty racist."

"Who cares? Racism is for white people to worry about."

"Okay, let's see: you like John because he's white and speaks English, and he can make lots of money."

"English is everything these days, you know that. He's a native speaker, that's enough of a reason to marry him."

"What if he's a creep? I heard he got divorced twice and he's got children from other families. He's a deadbeat. That's why he's here all alone. Where else can he get so much respect?"

"Even if John wasn't a professor, he could be working for one of those shady rent-a-white-guy companies. I think he's doing a real service by teaching."

"You're just coming up with excuses. I don't want to hurt your feelings, but you sound a bit dumb, like you're falling victim to mass media and white supremacy."

"There you go again, talking a bunch of nonsense I don't understand."

In a huff, the young student released Apple's arm and walked quickly ahead, until she came to row of vendor carts.

"Hey, I want a jianbing, want to split one?" the young student asked her friend, shouting behind her.

The young student loved jianbing, which were flat, hot, fried patties covered with green onions and garlic. Even more than jianbing, she liked eating raw green onions, big stalks of it dipped in huangdou jiang. Back home in Shandong she would eat dinner with flatbread in one hand, and a stalk of big, crispy green onion in the other, taking bites in turn.

She swallowed in anticipation as she watched the jianbing cook drag the batter in circles with his metal spatula, spreading it over the enormous round hot plate.

Presently, a foreigner came out of the school gate and walked toward them.

"Oh, look, it's John," said the young student.

As they were watching him, a pair of students, both female, walked toward him. The young student could not hear what was being said. But she could see the two girls giggling, taking turns snapping photos with John. The teacher smoothed his hair and brushed his bangs to one side. He stood straight, assuming a serious pose.

The two giggling students had just left when a sleek white car pulled up. A young woman dressed in a power suit with a plunging neckline and padded shoulders emerged and greeted John. The woman was a mystery to the young student. Possibly the woman was the daughter of a Taiwanese tycoon, who had come to visit the professor, who was her boyfriend. The car drove off, leaving the female student and Apple standing in the dust.

Life was unfair. The female student frowned and sighed. She wondered if she should just accept her lot and marry a decent, local boy.

"All this talk about John is bad for your brain," Apple said. "We can have fun on our own. But first, do you think fifty yuan is enough to buy glasses?"

Yes, it was, on Taobao. But if Apple made an online purchase, they wouldn't have an excuse to go off-campus and possibly look at more handsome foreigners downtown.

Normally they went to the city to buy snacks, to watch a movie, to patronize a fancy restaurant beyond their budget or even visit the cheaper clothing and accessories flea market. But here was a legitimate reason for the young student to go.

"Remember that eyeglass shop that we went into once?" the young student said. "That time we were looking at sunglasses? The store clerk really likes me, remember? I bet I could get him to give us a big discount."

The clerk was actually the owner of the eyeglass shop, a young, earnest bachelor. Instead of treating his intentions seriously, she planned to lead him on in order to save some money, all the while pining after her foreign teacher. That was a testament to the sorry state of affairs in the country.

The eyeglass shop was at the apex of two streets that intersected at an odd angle. The streets were densely packed and lined with shops at the base of low-rise apartments. It was the old part of town, and the streets were poorly maintained. Scruffy, barrel-chested men sat by the stoplights on tricycle carts, waiting to be hired. In the shops, wielders and artisans toiled away in their chosen occupation. The eyeglass shop looked relatively new, with its inventory nicely laid out in display cases around the store.

The shop clerk was indeed a young man with a clean haircut, wearing a casual dress shirt. What was not to like about him? Wasn't he handsome enough for her? Because of the gender ratio in the country, this single man would not have many chances to find a soulmate. The young student knew she should remember this fact.

"Hey, so you're still here?" She looked around the shop, everywhere but at the shop clerk.

"Yeah, oh yeah," the shopkeeper said, nearly drooling.

"My hair grew longer, I thought you might not recognize me." She turned around ostensibly to show off her hairdo, but instead she was giving him a good look at her figure.

Apple tried on a few eyeglasses and found a pair she liked. "Do I look good in this one?"

"Hey, can you give my friend a good deal on these?"

"Sure, of course," he said.

Toward the back of the store there was a chair and an eye examination chart. He gave Apple a sight test. Afterward, he went to the counter and computed the cost.

"Well, with the lenses, it'll be two hundred yuan total."

"Two hundred?" she said, blinking in disbelief. All that while, she had thought that this man who liked her would swoon and lose his mind over pretty looks, and hand out a free lunch, or, in this case, a free pair of eyeglasses. But, no, he was a respectable young local man. Exactly the kind of man she should not be leading on.

Stumped, and exposed for their unethical behaviour, the young female student muttered. The business transaction was off. In a moment, the students were both out on the street, without having made a purchase, and having lost face.

"What a stingy guy," she said. "Don't worry, you can buy eyeglasses on Taobao. Now we know your prescription." The morning was not wasted; they had learned Apple's prescription for free.

While downtown, it seemed a waste not to enjoy the day. "Let's go get our ears cleaned," she said. The ear shop was nearby, facing the street with a patio-style door. Inside were some straw living room chairs and a coffee table. Everything was white and pink, with some magazines and a teakettle and tea set. In the back was a narrow staircase.

Up the stairs the two friends went, making a loud thumping noise as they ascended. On the upper level, the small rooms had reclining chairs spaced apart, covered with white cloths.

They relaxed, drank tea and forgot their worries, as was the purpose of their visit. The students sat down in the comfortable chairs, which reclined so far back they were almost lying down.

Soon they were feeling the skilled hands of the attendant kneading their shoulders and neck. The country was full of these little pleasures. To think, if she fell in love with a foreigner and went abroad, she wouldn't have access to such excellent service. And that would mean throughout the year, especially in chilly weather when one's muscles were tense, she would have no one to help her unwind. This argument in itself was almost enough to convince the young student to abandon her plan to seduce her foreign teacher.

After the massage she was resting and feeling like putty. Another woman came in, wearing a face mask, pushing a little cart with tools on it. She had a miner's lamp strapped to her head.

"I'll go first," she said to Apple. "I probably need it more; I always have really dirty ears." The young female student lay there feeling the steel pick prodding her ear canal.

Soon enough, it was Apple's turn and they switched seats. While waiting, the young student watched the small TV hanging on the wall. When advertisements came on, they featured handsome male foreigners. No matter which way she turned she ran into images like these. The only way to deal with the matter was by changing her inner thinking, something that felt impossible to her.

To take her mind off the TV, she looked out the window. But to her surprise, she saw a vehicle like the one that had picked up her English teacher on campus. In fact, it was the exact same car. It pulled into a parking spot. The car door opened and her professor John appeared.

"What's he doing here?"

"What are you talking about?" Apple said.

"Wait a minute, okay? Stay here and finish your ear cleaning, I've got to go outside."

She was terrified, but at the same time something drew her to him. Was he coming for an ear picking? But no, that would be absurd, since the dirty Americans never liked to have their ears cleaned.

Outside, the professor spotted her, the young student. "Hello there," he said. "I know you."

"Oh, hello, Professor. I'm have ear cleaned."

"Ear cleaning?" John said, and he clapped his hands. "I'm having a tea, want to come in for a drink?" She was with her friend Apple, but Apple would be another twenty minutes, so what was the harm?

She entered the tea shop next door, tinkling the bell. It was a fancy tea shop that she had never set foot in before.

"My guide recommended this place," said John. The elegant woman who had accompanied John before appeared behind them, out of the car.

"She your guide?"

The elegant woman nodded. "Yes," she said in their native language. "I'm just showing him around the city. How do you know John?"

"He's my teacher."

"He's handsome, isn't he?" Together they giggled. "I'm only his guide for this month, his first month at this school. But you get him for the whole year, lucky you."

"Your English must be very advanced."

"Actually, just so-so, probably yours is better."

"Are you sure you're not his girlfriend or wife?"

The guide laughed, and announced that she was already married. To the young female student's delight, the guide informed her that John was unattached. But to be honest, the notion that she could be with such a handsome superstar like John was far-fetched. The information that he was single was more like a dog whistle far away, out of hearing range.

Nevertheless, she sat down with John in a cubicle and shared a tea serving ceremony, while the guide went to the restroom. Before the professor had never paid attention to her. However, now that he was so close, his eyes kept wandering over her face.

The student wasn't pretty enough to be a Taobao model, but perhaps she was attractive enough for him. After all, she had a pleasant complexion, not too dark, unblemished. She still had that youthful zest of a child, and her bright wide eyes were attractive. She had a cute nose, and a round, firm behind, which no doubt attracted foreign men.

She could hardly believe she was sitting down with the professor, directly across from him. When the waitress came, the student translated. In a way, she felt responsible for him. He was helpless, couldn't even order a tea without her. She felt a motherly affection for him.

Apropos of nothing, he asked, "Do you have a boyfriend?" Was it a hint that he was interested in her? Or was he just teasing?

She shook her head. "No, my parents don't allow it."

"That's too bad, a real shame."

"Doesn't matter. I don't listen them anyway."

"You don't?" His eyebrows jumped up. "Well, I'm sure there's someone you like."

"Me? No." She giggled, turning her eyes away.

"You should come to my apartment, have extra lessons."

Had she heard him correctly? She got very excited, unable to keep her imagination in check.

"Do you have wife?" she asked. "Or girlfriend? Your guide said no, but I didn't believe her."

He grinned and shook his head. "Once upon a time I did," he said. "Long, long ago." He chuckled, at what she did not know.

Then just like that her phone rang. It was Apple, asking for her. She was done with her ear cleaning.

"Oh, I'm so sorry," the young student said to John. "I need go, bye bye."

"Wait. Here's my phone number, if you're free tomorrow or this week, come over, okay?"

As improbable as it was, she had managed to snag him. Outside Apple took her by the arm. "What was that about?"

She told her what happened, breathless. "You're not pulling my leg?" Apple said. Later, Apple was still skeptical, but in a different way.

"You know, these foreigners are all playing the field. They can get any girl they want."

"He really likes me, I can see it in his eyes."

"Maybe I should go with you to his apartment, you could be really easy to trick, you know," Apple said. It was a generous offer, made obviously for the benefit of the young female student's security. But she wasn't worried. The foreign man was a professor. The worst thing that could happen was a kiss, and even that didn't bother her.

What did worry her was that perhaps her friend Apple's intentions were not pure. Maybe there was something else Apple wanted, like usurping her position with John.

"Don't worry, Apple, I'll be okay on my own," she said. "I'll call and let you know how it goes."

During class, when other girls sighed and swooned over the professor, the young student seemed nonchalant, appearing to have lost all interest.

Finally, the big day came. She picked out a special outfit, her best, most enticing dress. It was blue, with bows on the shoulders, and a frilly skirt. She went over to John's apartment. John opened the door, patting himself on the stomach. "I'm happy you could come."

"Me too, so happy," she said.

Inside it was fairly nice. Spacious, with two bedrooms, a courtyard in the back, complete with a kitchen and a living area. In this place, she could see herself as his wife. After she sat down on the white couch, in front of a glass coffee table, he brought her a cup of water.

"So, extra lessons are two hundred yuan an hour," he said. "I always get the money first."

Did she hear him correctly? She could not understand his meaning.

Embarrassed, not knowing what else to do, she took out her purse. But she did not have enough cash.

"It's okay." John smiled. "You can pay by WeChat."

She spent half an hour studying from a textbook while he paced back and forth by the window, spouting a bunch of English vocabulary she could not understand. "Repeat after me," he said. "Yellow butter, purple jelly, red jam, black bread. Spread it thick, say it quick." Now and then John let out a little laugh.

The young student breathed a sigh of relief when John put down the book. It was almost time to go. The young student felt so bad, hot all over. She had lost face, having bragged to her friend about being invited over to John's home.

"Thanks for coming over," John said, extending his hand.

She took his hand, and in a moment of inspiration, she pulled it to her chest so that he was touching her. She had never imagined herself possible of doing such a thing. She did not even know what it could mean, other than the fact that she had seen in a movie once that men liked to touch women's chests.

"Wh-What are you doing?"

"Kiss, kiss, kiss." She brought her mouth to his, pressing her face to his. Finally, she felt his body give way to her embrace. She felt like a little child holding onto a big giant.

"You're a little whore, aren't you?" She didn't know what the words meant, but she took them for affection. "Okay, you know what will be fun, if you take off your dress. Let me take some photos of you."

He held out his hand. It was really happening. The young student's heartbeat quickened. For the last hour, she had been biting her lip, crying inside, thinking she had embarrassed herself. Lucky for her, she had taken a leap, thrown herself on him. Now John, her teacher, finally realized he could act on his desires.

His hand was so big, with hairs sprouting from the backside of it. The young student's head spun.

"Take off that pretty blue dress. I want some photos of you, so I can send my buddies something fun."

She hesitated for a moment, but then she stared into his handsome face, and the young student began to take off her dress and brassiere. When he took out his phone and snapped some photos, she giggled and laughed.

"Good, just like that," said John. "Hold that pose. Good."

He made her pose in various humiliating positions: on a chair, under the table, with a carrot from the fridge, positioned in a suggestive way. Before their 'lesson' was over, he took off his pants and made her kneel in front of him. She went through certain motions, things he instructed. She didn't understand all of the words he said, but somehow she knew their meaning. In the end, she did as she was told. He seemed happy, and she was happy.

The next week, at school, as soon as she walked through the door, she knew something was terribly wrong. Everywhere she went, students turned away from her. Other students snickered when she walked by. They looked at their phones, and then at her. What were they looking at? She frowned and began to feel worried. Even her friend Apple avoided her and wouldn't reply to her WeChat messages. Finally, she was summoned to the dean's office.

"I won't mention the kind of repulsive habits you have become known for. But it is the duty of this office to expel you. The matter has already been decided, and this meeting is just a formality. If I had my way, you would be thrown in a swamp for disgracing our school with your lewd pictures."

She was crying as she left the campus, her mascara running down her face. She looked back one last time at the building where she had her classes. There she saw John, standing above, on the third-floor open hallway, facing the courtyard, watching her. She saw him wave, the corner of his lip tugging upward, before turning back to his class to begin his lecture.

7.
The Physics Problem

I SPOTTED HER ACROSS NANJING ROAD, WEARING A SUMMER dress. A few minutes later, at a stoplight, she crossed to my side of the street. I made an unremarkable comment about the weather almost to myself. She turned to speak. She was a bank teller and looked like a runway model. She was taller than me, slim, her delicate skin so pale her veins showed blue underneath. Farther down, in front of a Uniqlo, we sat on a bench flanked by a couple of trees. The sun was low and about to set. It was after work.

I don't remember much of what she said. She did strike me, in a superficial way, as one of those typical Shanghai girls, the spoiled bratty types who have good cooks for husbands. But like many other Shanghai women, she was educated and earned enough money on her own. I saw it in the way she dressed – designer labels, a fancy purse, which, no doubt, she'd bought for herself.

As for the rumour that Shanghai was the city – the only city – where everyone was happier to have a daughter than a son, I didn't know if there was any truth behind it. But I had heard people say such things. As tradition went, daughters could make money from marrying, whereas sons crumpled under too much pressure. Bride prices had risen because of the gender imbalance, especially in a wealthy, crowded city like Shanghai.

That day, she was sitting under a tree, with the evening sunlight behind her, casting a halo of yellow around her dark hair. In the breeze, a leaf fluttered down and landed on the top of her head, balancing there. She seemed not to notice, and because she looked both pleasant and absurd with the leaf resting on her hair, I laughed.

"There's a big leaf on your head, you know."

"Is there?" She looked up with her eyes, without moving her head. "Oh well." Then she continued talking, as if I hadn't mentioned the leaf. After a minute or two, another breeze came and swept the leaf away.

Four years passed. I had left the city and was in a bad – somewhat abusive – relationship, in a different part of the country, Jiangxi Province. I had tried to leave a few times. The last time, I packed half my things into my suitcase before I stopped. I simply couldn't finish. My hands kept trembling and I threw up.

But then, she began writing to me. She told me to come back to Shanghai. She wanted to spend some time with me. I read her words and simply walked out my apartment door and left.

I walked twenty minutes, halfway to the train station. There, on a patch of dry grass near a playground, I collapsed. Kids chased each other, jumping over me. The fear of being discovered, the possible violent consequences of my actions, had sucked the energy out of my body. I couldn't bring myself to go back to fetch my belongings. If I went back to get them, I wouldn't have it in me to walk out again. I would spend the rest of my life in that city, in that relationship.

The sun was so hot overhead. The shouting of children numbed my ears. I thought about the novel that I had handwritten in a notebook that I had left behind. I would have to rewrite it from the very first word. At least I remembered the title. The title I could keep.

I thought too about the city I was leaving. It was a small city, in the mountains. I would miss riding my scooter around the campus. I would miss spending days lost in the villages, among the fields. I liked to visit a cemetery hidden among the trees on the mountainside. Some afternoons, after class, I would get on my scooter and drive off-campus, down the long, lonely road, past the fields, until I reached the foot of the mountain. There, I drove along the narrow, winding lanes, past villagers, farmers, until I reached the cemetery gate.

The headstones were so old that the names and dates had worn off. There was never anyone around. I used to lie down among the graves, reading a book.

I would have stayed lying in the playground, with children jumping over me. I would have stayed until it grew dark, and I had missed my train. But fear took over. Fear of the woman I was leaving. Fear that someone she knew, one of her cruel relatives, would see me. I stood up and walked the rest of the way to the train station.

In Shanghai I found a hotel on the city outskirts with a spacious balcony overlooking the Huangpu River. Years later, thousands of pig carcasses would float down that same river, right outside my window, and make international news. But at the time all I saw were cargo ships, the blaring of sea horns.

I stood there, on the balcony, for hours, looking over the water, the fog. I had spent years in this country, wandering from city to city, running away, from what? A broken heart, a broken past. My sad history was like everyone else's. My answers, my excuses, were the same, just as boring.

That hotel turned out to be my favourite hotel in the city. Ordinarily, it would have been too expensive. But it was on the edge of the city and in the process of closing down. All but the eleventh and twelfth floors had been sold off and converted into long-term single-room rental units. The housekeeper was a friendly middle-aged woman with a mole on her face. Every day, she came by with her cleaning cart. For every towel I used, she would leave half a dozen fresh ones, as well as other unnecessary items. Apparently, their one-use supplies were in overabundance. Even the hotel staff did not know what to do.

I woke early in the morning before sunrise and walked about the neighbourhood, buying breakfast at a tiny shop that sold varieties of stuffed buns. I found a running track tucked behind a residential compound where older people took their morning strolls, and I joined them.

In the evening, there was a knock on the door. When I opened it, there she was. "Hi, Dan-ny," she said, pronouncing my name with Chinese tones. I hadn't seen her since that time on Nanjing Road. Her hair was longer, her face even more exquisite, in a different summer dress. In her hands was a takeout dinner she had bought for me. We didn't hug or shake hands, or kiss. She sat in the hotel chair, by the window, her knees together, saying nothing but looking at me with curious eyes. I remembered her personality. Her confidence and self-importance were replaced by something else. A hesitation that was hard to pinpoint.

We spoke for a short while. I was hoping that she would mend my heart, that we would become a couple. Presently she explained why she had written to me.

"I don't know how to say this but" – she hesitated – "I've never had sex. I'm a virgin."

I was baffled.

"But haven't you dated before?"

"I've had six boyfriends."

"Why are you telling me this?"

Her voice was pained. The notion was so ludicrous, and juxtaposed with my own personal ordeal, I wanted to laugh.

"It just doesn't work."

"What doesn't work?"

"No matter what I try, it doesn't happen."

"What exactly do you mean?" I asked. She shook her head, squirming and looking away. "Have you tried a vibrator?"

"What's that?"

"It's a kind of machine, I guess. A toy shaped like a banana. You use it like a penis."

"Gross. I just want to do it the proper way."

"I still don't understand: How could it not work?" I believed her, but I couldn't think of how it was possible.

"I don't know." She slouched her shoulders.

Whatever I asked, she would find a way to avoid answering my question. I pursued the issue, but with no better understanding. She came over the next night and the night after that. All we did was sit in the hotel and talk about her mysterious problem. Finally, she suggested that I try it with her.

"Are you okay with that?" she asked. "I don't want a relationship, I just want to get it over with. I want to see if I can do it."

"Sure," I told her. "I'd be honoured." Not once since I had moved into that hotel room had my mind wandered back to the painful time in Jiangxi, to the ugly life that had destroyed parts of me I didn't even know about yet. I was so grateful for this distraction that I would have married her. But also, I knew exactly how beautiful she was. She was angelic, almost elfin. The way she carried herself everywhere with a straight back.

While she was readying herself in the bathroom, I stood by the balcony, looking out the window. I thought about what would happen. I tried to imagine various scenarios in which it, her problem, was plausible. But nothing came to mind.

She came out and was about to slip under the covers, but I stopped her. "Shouldn't we kiss first? It seems strange to do that stuff without first kissing."

"I'm not sure I can."

"Don't worry, it's easy."

I turned off the light, put my hand around her and moved closer. In the last moment, she sucked her own lips into her mouth. She twisted her face away. In the shadows I could see her shape. I tried to kiss her by craning my mouth to meet hers. But she held it out of reach.

"Hold still," I said.

"Mam mam." Her voice was muffled by her contorted, inverted lips.

I didn't know why she was playing this trick on me. I tried a second time, making sure to be slow and gentle. But her head shook back and forth. The closer my mouth came to hers, the more violently she shook her head.

"What was that?" I rolled away and turned on the lights. She relaxed.

"What? What's wrong?"

"If you don't want to kiss, it's fine."

"Okay, the kissing part isn't important. Let's get to it." She burrowed under the covers.

I was a little spooked. Before turning off the lights, I lifted the blanket and took a look at her anatomy. It wasn't something I normally did, but I was a bit nervous. I figured there must be some physical explanation for her problem. However, when I took a look down there, everything was in order.

"Take off your pants." She gestured at my crotch.

Under the blanket, with the lights off, but with the late-day sun filtering through the curtain, I removed the last of my clothing. Disrobed, I tried a few typical manoeuvres that I thought would help her feel ready, but she stopped me. "I don't like that stuff." She shook her head. So I hovered over her and took a deep breath.

The moment I got close to her, within an inch or two, her waist and hips began to swing from side to side, as if the bed was on fire.

"Hold still." I placed my hands on her.

"I am."

I tried a second time. Her lower body began to shake. The closer I got, the more wildly her hips jerked back and forth.

"What is going on? Don't you realize what you're doing?" She looked distraught and disappointed.

"Is it normal?"

"Normal?" I blinked. I didn't know what qualified as normal. I didn't want to hurt her feelings. I thought about the six guys before me and felt a newfound fraternity. "It's really just a physics problem," I said, a question in my voice.

This time, I held her tightly, careful not to hurt her. There was no problem with her upper body. But her bottom half was like some strange deep ocean creature, twisting and turning as if she were made of stretchy rubber putty. But then everything changed. Something was pushing at me.

When I looked down, I saw that her flesh was wriggling, as if the skin itself was a sentient being. As I watched, pods unfurled from her body, plantlike, engorged and scaly. They stretched, like tentacles, and crept upward, toward me. I counted three, and the longest one, purple and spotted, extended straight up, over my head. Finally, I felt the terror exploding in my gut and I scrambled off the bed.

"Oh god, what's that?"

"What?" she said. "What?"

"Your body," I stammered. I blinked and looked toward her again. She looked perfectly normal. "I-I- I don't know what that was. Was that painful?"

"Painful? No, why?"

"You had some kind of . . . uh . . . reaction to me," I said. "Have you seen a doctor? Maybe it was an allergy."

"I look okay now, don't I?" She lay down on the bed, still naked, and spread her legs apart. I looked at her carefully. Yes, she was her normal self now. But I knew I hadn't imagined it.

"But how?"

"You mean it's not supposed to happen like that?" I shook my head. I wondered about the six guys who had come before me.

What had their reactions been? Had they run, slamming the door, half-naked? I felt a pang of pity for how rejected she must have felt.

"Should we try it again?" she asked.

"No! We should go to the ER. Maybe a doctor can help."

She was crying a little, scared. "Don't worry," I lied, "it's pretty common."

"Is it? Is it curable?"

"Yes, I'm sure it's nothing. You just need some medicine."

We got a DiDi car. "Take us to the nearest hospital," I said to the driver. "No, wait, not a state hospital, a private one."

"What's wrong with the public hospital?" the driver snorted.

"Please, just find an expensive one."

"Is your friend okay?" He was looking in the mirror at her.

"I'm fine." She wiped her red eyes. "It's something I ate."

We arrived at the Shanghai National People's Private Hospital. It was well lit and clean. The admitting nurse led us to the gynecology department. Fortunately, a doctor was available, a young, modern woman. I felt hopeful as we explained the situation.

During the examination, I waited outside the office. I could hear muffled noises. Finally, the gynecologist opened the door and beckoned me in.

"How is she?"

"Your friend is perfectly healthy," the gynecologist said.

"But . . . how can that be?" I asked. "Did you confirm what I saw? The growths? The scaly skin, the pods?"

"Did she have pain?"

"No, I don't think so." I turned to my friend, who nodded.

"No pain," my friend said. "I'm fine. And the doctor says it's nothing to worry about." She looked relieved.

"It's her body's way of protecting itself."

"What do you mean?" I asked.

"Sex isn't possible, at least not for the time being. It's understandable, given the trauma that she experienced when she was in college. The effects can last for years, maybe even a lifetime."

I didn't understand. "Let me show you what happened, doctor. If you see it yourself, you'll be just as shocked as me." I wasn't sure how to trigger the effect. But I thought if my friend could lie down on the patient's table, and I could simulate the evening's activities, it would do the trick.

"I already examined her." The doctor held her arm out to block my way. "There's no need."

"Can't you give her some blood work, some more tests?"

"I can understand how this is confusing for you both, but this sort of thing does happen."

"What? The bizarre growths? It's impossible, there were tentacles. Her skin and flesh were wiggling and moving around like there was a squid inside her."

"Such graphic language isn't necessary." The doctor turned to my friend. "Is it all right if I explain to him?" My friend nodded and the doctor continued. "As I explained earlier, it's a normal function of the female condition. You see, inside her brain are deep memories from a past trauma. She may have forgotten, but the body remembers. When there is a sexual stimulus, the skin and blood vessels can spontaneously rearrange to form a protective matrix, which acts to keep external objects at a distance. This happens all the time at the cellular level. But it can happen at a macroscopic level too. Once the stimulus is removed, the body returns to its normal state. If you want to think of it as an allergy, you can. What I have already recommended is that she see a therapist to help treat the core issue, so that someday her body reacts differently. In any case, I wouldn't be alarmed. We've seen this sort of thing in many, many women."

We walked down the hall and sat down on a row of blue plastic chairs. "What were you two talking about in there? What happened in college?"

"A boy did something to me," she said. "I can't remember it too well. The doctor was asking about it."

"I've really never heard of anything like this."

We left the hospital and walked down the street. The fresh air made me feel better. "Do you want me to come with you to see the therapist?" I asked.

My friend shook her head. "I'm okay. Like the doctor said, it's nothing to be worried about. Maybe talking to a therapist will help me. Anyway, I've always wanted to have a therapist, this is a good reason."

We parted at an intersection. "I'd like to see you some more. What do you think? Will you meet me again?" She squeezed my hand and nodded.

"Meet me here tomorrow," she said.

When I looked back at her, across the street, she blew me a kiss.

Maybe it was a drop of rain, but something wet touched my cheek. A tightness in my chest, which I hadn't noticed before, seemed to give way. I rolled my shoulders back, and took a deep, satisfying breath, and my head spun with the extra oxygen. I looked up and saw darkening, merciful clouds above.

8.
The Blond Teacher

SEVERAL STUDENTS HAD FALLEN IN LOVE WITH THE BLOND-haired, blue-eyed teacher in the first two months of her working at the school as a foreign teacher. She was the first female foreigner the school had hired, and everybody hoped she would not be the last. She had freckles and a cute, upturned nose. Moreover, she had a timid but graceful way of walking, like a gazelle. When she walked down the hall, she would place one foot directly forward, then the rest of her body would follow.

Of the students who loved her, none was more infatuated than a young male art student. He had never dated anyone before, let alone someone who looked like the beautiful foreign teacher. He hoped that one day she would return his feelings. After all, he thought, he was a friendly person. He had a social circle and came from a respectable family.

He had his own car, given to him by his parents, who were professional, white-collar people, both teachers in a public school. Although it was ratty and old, having a car was a status symbol in the town where they lived.

Her name was Elena, but the school had christened her Mary. Everyone suspected she was from Russia because of the way that she spoke, but the school declared she was from Britain. The art student felt she was his soulmate, the perfect muse for his work. He decided that the first thing he would do with her, when they were together, was pose her in his studio with a backdrop of roses and sunlight. He wanted to make a real-life portrait of her, as life-like as possible, to capture her essence.

Unsure how to approach her about his feelings, he asked two classmates to help, one named Jason and the other named Santo, names they only ever used in their English class.

"Can you get her phone number for me?" he asked.

"I can try," said Jason. "But why do you want it?"

"I want to be friends with her. I want to tell her how I feel."

"What's your feeling exactly?" Santo asked.

"It's like . . . there's a rainbow in my stomach." He didn't know how to describe it, so he settled for this far-fetched, meaningless image, hoping it would impress his friends.

"I don't think a phone number's any use," Jason said. "What will you say to her? Your English isn't all that good. Not good enough to have a decent conversation. And won't you be too nervous to talk?"

"I do get nervous easily," the young art student admitted.

"Well, then, what about contacting her using messages? You can type better than you can speak, right?" Jason pantomimed typing with his hands held out in front of him.

"And what about emojis?" Santo suggested. "If you find yourself tongue-tied, or don't know how to express yourself, just pick a smiley face or a frowny face."

"Just ask for her WeChat. It's all I need to start."

The two friends found the female teacher in the stairwell the next day. "Do you have a boyfriend?" Jason asked her. She laughed and shook her head.

"Do you have WeChat?" Santo added.

"Yes," said the beautiful teacher. "I have it, but I don't use it much. Why?"

"Can you give your WeChat for us?"

"Okay, sure."

But when the two friends wrote to her, they discovered that she did not reply to any messages. There were, as it turned out, other students who had asked for her contact information, and soon word spread that it was pointless.

"She probably doesn't know how to use WeChat," Santo guessed. "Someone has to teach her."

"She's too busy, or she doesn't want to use it," Jason said, shrugging.

The art student listened to this gossip, uncertain how to solve his dilemma. He began to watch from across the street. He soon learned the time that Mary left the school every day. Someone like her had enough money to take a taxi or hire a driver. But the odd thing was that she would walk down the street and wait at the bus stop.

The art student got into his car and waited by the side of the road. When he saw her walking along the street to the bus stop, he pulled up to her.

"Hey, it's me," he said, through the open window across the passenger-side seat. "Get in, okay?" He waved his hand. From inside the dark car, he could see her squint, trying to see who he was. Sensing her hesitation and fear, the art student became frustrated. She didn't understand his English, even though he had practised and had made an extra effort to speak clearly.

He spoke some more, asking this time for her WeChat. He could tell that she didn't understand the sounds he was making. He gestured wildly, trying to help her comprehend his words with his hands, but she only stepped back, her face frozen in an expression of confusion and fear. He could not understand her apprehension. She was so friendly in class. She always had a smile for him and for other students. Finally, he shouted angrily. He hit the steering wheel with his hand. In an excess of emotion, he drove off with a screech of tires and a puff of black smoke.

During lunch the next day, the art student watched to see where Mary went. She usually bought a bag of chips, or had a Starbucks drink or fast food. He followed her to a shop by the nearby river that served noodles. She walked up and down the street a few times, seemingly unsure of which shop to try. Wherever she walked, the people on that quiet street would follow her with their heads, their eyes, sometimes pointing with their fingers. Men sat on stools together, playing chess or chatting, and they stopped everything as she approached. They looked at her, turning in their seats as she passed by. She poked her head into the noodle shop. A moment later, she left, with a little steamed bun in a brown paper bag.

On the way back, instead of going back to the school, she went across the street to a piano shop facing the road. There, another student was waiting outside. The art student knew her by reputation – she was a master's candidate at the Shanghai music conservatory. She could play all the instruments: the guzheng – a long big one with strings, dizi, even erhu. Once she was even on TV.

He watched as the two hugged and went inside. He stood, left behind, on the sidewalk, on the opposite side of the road. He could see golden hair shimmering in a second-floor window. He heard the blond teacher's laughter and the sound of a piano. He listened to them play a tinkling duet, "Dance of the Sugar Plum Fairy." He had always hated sweets.

Since the frustrating incident when he had spoken to Mary from his car, he had avoided going to the school, spending his days at home instead, mixing paints on a palette until they formed a murky, mud-like goo. He didn't know how to proceed. Then, his luck changed. One weekend there was a birthday party at the house of another teacher, and the beautiful blond teacher was to attend.

The art student arrived early to find the apartment full of loud and happy students and staff from the school. There was a keyboard and karaoke. Someone brought out a birthday cake and there was much singing and merriment. When the blond teacher arrived, she was mobbed by the students. They crowded around her to take photos and chat, and just to be close to her.

Perhaps it was the cake, the joy of being with so many happy people and the lovely music. But when someone asked for her WeChat, the blond teacher took out her phone.

"This is how you use WeChat," another student explained. "Make sure you add us."

The art student, timid, but methodical, added her contact to his phone and sent her an invitation.

"Add me," he said, pointing to her phone. He could see, from her happy and open expression, that she didn't know it was him who had called to her from the car. He waited beside her, with the other students standing there as witnesses. She laughed and clicked the add button. The art student went away happy.

He had wanted to wait a few days before writing her the first message. But he could not resist and sent a message that night. He waited a few minutes. When she did not reply, he sent another, and then another. They were a series of animated icons: tiny black-and-white images of a weird ghoul boy swaying back and forth, with long black hair that flopped over the face. He loved them.

He did not know or expect that when the blond teacher saw these icons, especially so late at night, she would be terrified. Why would he ever assume that a woman would fear him? He had never courted anyone before.

When still she did not reply, he became irritated and sent another image. This one showed a horrid, disfigured cartoon face, with lifelike flies darting out of the eyes and into the nostrils.

Finally, she replied.

"Stop sending me this stuff."

"Where are you?" he wrote. "Can we meet?"

"No, leave me alone."

He looked at the short message and felt cheated. He had hoped she would have replied with a long love letter. Perhaps a photo of herself in a nightgown, or whatever. He didn't know. But never in his imagination had he thought her reply would be so short and blunt.

He continued to follow her, parking his car around corners and in shadows, any hidden place he could find. One day, she took a different route home. "She's moved," he muttered to himself. "She got a new apartment." Keeping one hand on the steering wheel, he picked up his phone to write a message.

"Congratulations! How's your new home?" he started to write. But he remembered her last message and deleted it.

Instead, he kept following her until he saw her enter a concrete building, fifteen minutes away from campus. He took a photo of a church in the park, across the road. He sent the photo to her, without adding any text, thinking it was a good compromise.

There was a stone path from one end of the park to the other, curving everywhere. In the middle was a naturally shaped pond, lined with reeds, decorated with a few classic bridges. He sat for a while and watched a couple playing badminton under a tented area. Later he went to the basketball courts and watched young men playing basketball. Sports weren't something he enjoyed. He wondered how they could do that every day, so hot and sweaty.

The main feature of the park was the church. It was a big dome, the biggest in the city. Inside was grand, with stained-glass windows and wood carvings lining the ceiling at the front of the pulpit. Even though he didn't understand the idea of worship, the beauty of the place moved him.

"You can take a look, go inside," said a caretaker, who opened the heavy wood door for him.

Even the air seemed different, cooler, calmer, more at peace. The thick walls blocked the frenzied noises of the city. The art student stared in awe at the enormous, towering figures carved in the walls. For a long time he sat on a pew at the front, undisturbed by anyone, simply gawking from one end of the great room to the other.

After a while, the pastor appeared, a balding man in a cloak.

"Would you like to join our congregation? If you're free on Sunday morning or Tuesday afternoon, please stop by again so that you may rejoice in the word of God."

The art student had no idea what the pastor was talking about, but goosebumps came up on his arms.

"Do you enjoy music?" the pastor asked. "We have a choir and an organist."

The art student shook his head. "I like art," he said.

"All around you is art. It's the art of God."

The art student looked up and around, and was indeed impressed by the majesty of the hall.

"Come again on Sunday. You will meet many people. We are all God's children."

He left the pastor, slipping out of the heavy wood door. In the church courtyard were sculptures and figurines of Christ and Mary and a scene of a stable, and the student stopped to trace his finger along the crude, wooden edges. As he straightened up, he saw a foreign woman pass by.

She looked like the blond teacher. She was young. Her hair was sandy brown, not blond, but she was beautiful as well. She walked by without looking at him. He ran up and stopped her.

"Hi, hello," he said.

She regarded him warily.

"Mary?" he said.

"No, I'm not Mary," she said, and walked on.

"Wait, hello? Do you know Mary?" he asked, following her.

"I don't know Mary. Sorry, I'm in a hurry."

She walked quickly away from him. He followed her for a minute or two, hoping she would turn around and talk to him. But she didn't. She left the park and got into a car. He stood at a distance, watching the car leave.

"I'm across the road from you, in the park," he wrote to Mary. "Want to come out for a walk?"

He waited a full two minutes, and still there was no answer. Infuriated, he tapped out a bunch of violent GIFs: knives, flames, skulls and crossbones. He pressed the send button. The message failed. A little red arrow popped up. He had been blocked. He tried a few more times, but the red arrow popped up again.

There's got to be some mistake, he thought.

He wrote to Santo, his classmate.

"There's something wrong with Teacher's WeChat," he said. "Can you send her a smiley face?"

"What? Just a smiley face?"

"Yes," he said. "See if it goes through. I think her WeChat is broken."

A minute later, Santo replied, "It went through."

When the art student got to school the next day, the principal asked to see him, holding out a printed report.

"If you don't stop contacting this teacher, we'll have to suspend your enrolment."

"It's all just a misunderstanding. I didn't know she felt that way."

"I really hope so. Control your feelings and don't do anything that would disgrace yourself or the school."

"Do what most men do," Jason said. "Propose to her in a public place and make sure all your friends are there. We'll all yell at her to marry you. She won't be able to take the pressure. She'll say yes. Look, I'll show you a video of a guy who did this exact thing in another city."

The idea appealed to him. He was a bit hesitant only because there was the chance, small though it might be, that she would say no. He didn't enjoy being publicly humiliated.

"Yes, you're right. If I can publicly express my devotion to her in front of all my friends, she'll realize I'm sincere, that I respect her, that I'm not playing around. She'll feel proud that I'm giving her so much face."

"You can count on me. I'll round up all our old school chums."

"But where should we do it?"

"How about Changning Mall? That's the most public place in the city. Just remember to get a suit and buy a ring first."

He went home, nervous. He lived in a one-bedroom apartment on the third floor – his bedroom was a painting studio, and he slept on a cot in the living area – in a big building in the older part of the city. From the floor above, the student often heard sounds of fighting. That night, staying up to work on his portrait of the beautiful blond teacher, he heard footfalls, like a dozen or more people were scuffling about. He heard a woman screaming, wailing, and fast feet running back and forth, a body being dragged, kicking, furniture toppling, begging and pleading and a man yelling above it all.

How horrible it would be to have a love like that, the art student thought.

Even with all the noise, he finished Mary's portrait. In his eyes, the painting was still not as good as he wanted it to be. He had posed her in front of a group of students, whose faces were all smeared out. Only her face was distinct, and her blue eyes glowed, open wide. But it wasn't quite right, as if he couldn't quite capture her essence, what made her unlike every other woman he had ever met. But he had no more time, and he was confident she would like it as it was.

The next morning, at school, he saw the blond teacher's friend, the music student, walking down the hall. He followed her, watched her walk into the women's bathroom and, looking to make sure no one else could see, entered behind her. Her bag was on the counter. Quickly, he reached in and stole her phone. He hurried back into the hall. The phone was unlocked and he sent a message.

"Want to come listen to my pipa show?" he wrote. He sent her the address of the public square, next to the most popular shopping mall. Hundreds of passersby would witness his proposal. "It is tonight, please come if you can. It's free."

Instead of returning the phone to the music student, he dismantled the battery and dropped it in the wastebasket beside the vending machine.

At the jewellery store, he found a ring he liked right away. "She's going to love it, and it's affordable." The female clerk winked and held it out for him to examine. The heart-shaped centre was set with a sparkling cubic zirconia, flanked on either side with what appeared to be moonstones. The band itself was made of sterling silver.

"Are the stones imported?"

"No, but the company that made it is called Susubangé. It's French-sounding. Look, here's the box." She showed him a tiny, velvet box. "See, no Chinese characters anywhere. This one is as good as any import."

After paying for it, he went into the flower shop next door.

"How much for flowers?" he asked. He had never bought flowers for anyone before. Now here he was with an engagement ring, looking for a bouquet, about to propose marriage. Whatever amount, he was willing to spend. "What flowers do girls like?"

"Roses," said the shopkeep. "You should buy at least half a dozen."

"She's the kind of woman who deserves the best."

"You have to make a good impression on the parents. Most parents like tradition, and when the time comes, you should get something for the parents too."

"Like what?"

"Well, cigarettes for the father, of course, and maybe some Blue Sky gin. For the mother, well, there's any number of things, as long as it's good quality. You should ask if her parents are very traditional."

"Actually, she's not Chinese."

"Oh no?"

"She's from abroad, she's beautiful, with long, blond hair. I'm proposing to her tonight."

"Take this, it's the biggest one I have, ninety-nine roses – longevity for your love. Just be careful, there're lots of sharp thorns on the stems."

The young art student held the bouquet, which was wrapped in blue. He had never held so many flowers, bundled together. "Yes," he nodded, "I think this is just what I need."

"I hope after you settle down with her, you'll bring her by the mall. I'd like to take a look at her."

The shimmering blue foil of the bouquet was like the colour of her eyes.

That afternoon, when the foot traffic in the area was at its peak, the young art student arrived at the city square. Jason had already assembled a small army of young men, some of whom the art student didn't even know or recognize.

"We'll wait for her to come," Jason said. "Everyone will form a circle around her, and we'll play the proposal song on the boom box and start the dance routine. After he asks her the big question, I'll lead the chant, 'Marry him! Marry him!' Don't stop shouting, otherwise she'll have second thoughts."

"Thanks so much, everyone. I really appreciate it," the young art student said.

"Make sure you get down on one knee. Women are all traditional. Once they see that you've got down on one knee, they'll know they have no choice. They'll have to say yes because you've put her on a pedestal. Every woman likes to be on a pedestal."

Jason handed out wedding candies, which they planned to throw into the air at the celebratory moment.

The young art student went to the mall entrance, where he stood looking out over the square, looking for the beautiful blond teacher.

"I don't see her," he said.

"Did you tell her to look for you by the flagpole? Wait. There she is!"

Jason pointed out the double doors. The foreign teacher, her blond hair teased by the breeze, was wearing a pink summer dress decorated with flowers, and high-heeled shoes. She walked slowly to the centre of the square, turning her head, looking around. The young art student saw her. Her beauty made him catch his breath.

As they had arranged, a group of young men quickly surrounded her. Even at a distance, the young art student could see the puzzled expression on Mary's face. They could hear the music now blaring, and saw the young men doing their dance routine. The dancers stepped to one side, then the other, punching their arms out in time. Their heads angled back as they skipped on their toes, before they did a cool move to either side with their hands, like they were chopping onions.

"It's time, let's go," shouted Jason. The young art student followed his friend out the doors. Under the sun, he licked his dry lips. There was something in his mouth. He spat, but couldn't get it out. He wiggled his finger on his tongue and pulled out a black hair, which he flicked away.

As they reached the group, the music stopped and the dancers parted to let him through. He could feel all their eyes on him. He was aware of the spectators and passersby who had crowded around. He reached the threshold and saw her, now face to face. Her expression seemed so pure, smiling mouth and bright eyes. It occurred to him that she might have thought that the music student had organized this delightful surprise for her. When she recognized him, her face transformed, collapsed into itself, became smaller somehow and full of wrinkles.

The young art student pulled the bouquet of flowers out from behind his back. He bent down on one knee.

He tried to say the words he had rehearsed the night before, but he was so nervous.

"Teacher Mary," he said, "wait a moment." He pulled out a crumpled piece of paper and unfolded it. Slowly, with careful pronunciation, he read from it: "After today, I won't call you 'Teacher' again. I know you said no to me so many times. But today I want to show my feelings for you. I really hope you have as much courage as me, enough to say yes to my love. So" – he held out the ring in its open case – "will you marry me?"

The blond teacher took a step back, trembling. The look on her face turned to something indescribable, like she was trapped in a nightmare. She held both hands out, as if to ward off the people around her. At this point, all the men around started their shouting.

"Hey, marry him!"

"Marry him! Say yes! Say it!"

"I love you, Mary," the young art student said, still on one knee, looking up at her.

"Get up, stop this."

"Marry me, please." He stood up and took a few steps closer to her.

"No, I don't want to."

"Marry him, do it!"

The shouting redoubled, the men yelling even louder and more persistently. Strangers hurried over and joined in too. The din of the voices drowned out her objections. All the blond teacher could see were the faces of men furiously shouting at her. She saw their upraised arms, clenched fists, others holding phones pointed in her direction, recording everything.

"Marry him, marry him!"

"No!"

"Look, Teacher, I made this for you." The young art student beckoned to his friend. Jason carried over the canvas and propped it up in front of the blond teacher. The young art student pulled back the cloth cover, unveiling his work.

The beautiful blond teacher stared at the portrait. There she was, with wide, frightened eyes in cerulean blue. Painted hands emerged from the darkness and groped every part of her body. She stumbled back a few steps, frightened, but there was nowhere to go. She was blocked on all sides.

"You don't like it?" The young art student stuttered, his face flushed in the heat, with everyone looking. "I've thought about you, day and night. But it's not enough, is it?"

The blond teacher turned about, trying to kick off her high heels, but tripped and fell on to her hands and knees. With one punch, he destroyed his painting, his fist ripping through layers of oil paint and canvas, loose threads clinging to the sweat on his hand. As she tried to stand up, he grabbed the hair on the back of her head and pulled, until he could see her beautiful, unblemished face, red in the sunshine, red with fear. He thought he heard the crowd shouting, "Punch her, punch her," but it didn't matter. He would have done it anyway.

Part Three: Conquest

9.
The Birthday Party

THE YOUNG MAN AND THE YOUNG WOMAN, WHOSE NAME was Shu, got engaged the week before Shu's twentieth birthday.

The young man brought her to meet his parents in his hometown village before going to her hometown as well. After that, they had gone to see Huangshan, the famous Yellow Mountain. On the way back, Shu's school friend, Bo, met up with them. The three came back together on an overnight train ride to Shanghai.

On the platform, as they boarded the train, station employees sold snacks from carts. Shu ordered a bowl of hulatang, sour soup. "It's my birthday tomorrow, and I get to have my favourite," she said, breathing in the spicy fumes that tickled her nostrils.

Looking at her, the young man reflected on how they had met. He had never expected to marry an Anhui woman. After all, the province had been buried in poverty for generations due to historical reasons, including flooding and natural disasters. As it was a central spot in the country, soldiers and armies had passed through these lands time and again. The local people had learned to live bitter, difficult lives. Young people moved away and hustled for homes, jobs, well-off husbands. The young man wasn't rich. An Anhui woman would want more than he could give, or so he would have said if he had been asked.

He had first seen her in an industrial part of Shanghai. She was riding on the back of a motorcycle, wearing her dark factory jacket and shorts, her long, toned legs showing. She was hardly seventeen then, no more than a girl, looking far less innocent (her parents might have said) than she was. He was only five years older, but he felt like he had discovered and mentored her and that she ought to stay with him because of that fact. Everything was perfect. Except, he worried that she was too intelligent for her looks and too good-looking to stay with one man for long. But he knew better than to say these specific words out loud, especially to her.

"Don't wear such revealing clothing," he had said instead, at the beginning of their relationship. "That shirt is cut too low."

"But it's the new style."

"It's not appropriate for you."

"I don't care what's appropriate."

"Please, you know Shanghai aunties like to gossip. They're all bagua, very nosey."

At first, she acquiesced. But after a year or so, he noticed she was wearing whatever she liked.

"I told you not to dress like that," he snapped.

She half-heartedly listened and made some attempts to appease him. But after a while she started ignoring him. She didn't fight back, she just laughed at his suggestions. He was at a loss. As much as he had tried to get her pregnant, it hadn't seemed to work, and when he asked if he was doing something wrong to prevent a baby, she only shrugged and wouldn't answer. Finally, fearing he would lose her, and not knowing how else to attach himself to her, he proposed marriage. He was surprised she said yes, but he hid it well and kissed her instead.

On the train Shu watched a foreign film on a cheap tablet device. It was a Hollywood film, starring a handsome movie star.

"Why do you always watch this garbage?"

"They're well made," Shu replied.

Bo chuckled. "You mean the movies or the actors?"

"Don't be stupid," said the young man.

"Hey, don't get upset at me," said Bo. "I'm not the one you have to worry about. I'm too short for her, isn't that right, Shu?"

"Yes, Bo, you're a midget, really. I like tall men."

The young man pushed his chest out. He was aware of his height, pleased with it.

"I would never be able to steal her from you," said Bo. "But maybe when we get back to Shanghai, she'll meet a taller, handsome foreigner."

"Oh, Bo." Shu snuffed down her nose.

Inside the train, their doorless cabin contained three hard bunks, stacked one above the other. The uppermost ones were so high and close to the ceiling that when the young man laid down to see which bunk he wanted, his hot breath bounced back into his face. He couldn't get away from his own smell. These were, of course, the cheapest tickets, apart from single seats.

The train moved along while Shu finished watching her foreign film. The young man rested on the bottom bunk with his fiancée curled up next to him, Bo snoring above. There was no room to move and he had to lie on his side, but it was better than sleeping with the ceiling four inches from his nose.

She was breathing very lightly, regularly. Possibly she had already dozed off. The young man drifted off into an uneasy sleep; he kept waking as the train's wheels rumbled underneath. In the dark, his brain circled back to Shu. *I love her so much*, he thought, before drifting back to sleep. Close to dawn, he woke again and she was no longer beside him.

"Shu?" he tentatively called out. He pushed himself up on his elbow. Perhaps she had gone to the bathroom.

The lights in the train had been turned off. The windows were black. He waited, listening to the rhythmic thudding of the train as it sped through the night. For a long time, he waited, until he got up himself, somewhat irritated, and carefully climbed out of the bunk.

At the end of the train car, he spotted her at the gangway, standing with two strangers.

The two strangers were smoking cigarettes outside the bathroom. Perhaps Shu had gone to use the toilet and then struck up a conversation with them. One was an older Chinese man. The other was a foreigner, a white man, about fifty years old. This foreigner was not particularly handsome. But he had a fine, dignified face, with oval-shaped eyeglasses, and a rather round nose and belly.

Mostly the young man looked at his fiancée. "She's flirting with him, it's obvious," he muttered.

He watched for a while longer. Then, without letting her see him, the young man went back to the cabin and slipped into his bunk, angry and trembling. He lay awake until she came back finally, on her own. He kept his eyes closed and pretended to be asleep. He knew without looking that the night outside the window was a bluish-black, an eerie sort of colour.

In the morning the passengers woke up bright and early. The sun was shining through the curtain. The harsh fluorescent lights were turned on. The train plodded forward, stopping now and then due to delays. It rolled along the tracks, passing by low brick shanty houses, then large shiny buildings and busy, traffic-jammed roads. Like this, sometime in the afternoon, they arrived in Shanghai.

As the young man was collecting his belongings, he noticed his mobile phone was missing.

"Are you sure you brought it with you?" Shu asked.

"What colour is it?" Bo made a show of patting down his own pockets.

"White." The young man frantically pushed aside some keys and sanitary napkins in Shu's purse. "It's got a white case."

They got off the train, onto the crowded platform. Around them were modern high-speed trains and old classic locomotives, which trudged slowly into the station, screeching and whining to a stop with puffs of smoke.

The trains were mostly packed with the same type of passengers: men wearing dark-green dusty coats, migrant workers from poor rural villages who had come to the city to make money. They had wrinkled faces, nervous eyes, each of them peering out the windows, neither waving nor smiling, nor betraying what they thought of what the world had become.

On the floor above, in dozens of massive rooms and station hallways, travellers waited for trains. Crowds, hundreds upon hundreds of city folk and migrants from around the country, stood or sat against the wide terminal walls.

Waiting in the line to get off the platform, the young man saw the foreigner from the previous night, with whom Shu had been speaking.

He probably thinks he's having a lovely time taking the trains, the young man thought. *He'd better stay away from me.*

The young man saw something that made him catch his breath. In the foreign man's hand was a shiny white mobile phone. An illogical, almost impossible idea, gripped the young man. He pushed his way over.

"Hey, what's that in your hand?" the young man shouted in Chinese, pointing at the phone.

The foreigner stepped around the young man. "Get away," he said, in English.

"The phone in your hand, it's mine. Give it to me. I know you understand Chinese!"

The foreigner stared. His facial expressions sent the young man into even more of a rage.

"What, this?" the foreigner said, getting the drift of the accusations. "You ass. You think this is yours?"

He held out the phone. The young man saw it was a brand new iPhone, totally unlike his Huawei. A moment later, the foreigner was gone. The young man, embarrassed, wanted to chase after him. He wanted to claw his head off, push him in front of a train.

People around were dispersing. He could hear the crowd snickering. Somehow, he knew that the foreigner had embarrassed him deliberately. He had been tricked into making a false accusation.

"What was that all about?" Shu came up behind him, her face flushed.

As they exited the station, the young man spotted the same foreigner entering the bathroom. The foreign man carried a suitcase and a black attaché case.

"Wait for me here, I need to use the bathroom," the young man said to his two companions.

Inside the bathroom, he saw the foreign man's bags by the sink. The foreigner was facing the urinal, his back turned. The young man opened the attaché case, undid his pants' zipper and relieved himself.

The young couple dropped their bags off and had a drink. That evening, together with a few friends, they headed out to a popular, upscale restaurant called Mr. Pot and Pan, intending to finish up the night with a late snack.

On the street, cars drove by, with motorbikes and bicycles weaving about, honking on all sides.

"I read about this restaurant online. It's supposed to be very good," Shu said.

As they sat down to eat, Bo thumped the table. "Hey, Shu's fiancé is paying tonight so order the best."

Shu's fiancé was not particularly in a humorous mood, and he scowled. Bo was putting his jacket on the chair when he pulled something out of the pocket. "Shu – take a look." Bo waved a white device in the air. "Your hubby's phone was in my jacket."

"How'd it get there?"

Bo shrugged. The young man took back his phone, grumbling as he did so.

But the food came, and all was well, all the more so because the dishes were delicious. Shu waved the waiter down, as a joke, and said, "I'd like some hulatang, please. Do you have it? It's my birthday."

Bo snickered behind his hand and whispered to the young man, "Her innocent act is convincing, no? Look at her, pretending to be a country girl who is so simple she orders street food at a respectable restaurant."

The waiter scratched his head nervously, unable to satisfy her request. The young man, Shu's fiancé, found it hard to join in the general merriment and laughter.

"She's from Anhui," shouted Bo. "You have to excuse her."

They ordered some cheap beer. They all drank. The young man watched as Bo finished bottle after bottle. *He'll start tormenting me again*, he thought.

"I just bought an excellent English textbook on Taobao," Bo said. "I highly recommend it. Shu, how's your English? Are you still studying?"

"Not really." She shrugged. "I don't like learning from books. I'm more of a hands-on learner."

"What a waste of time," said the young man.

"But, Shu, do you agree that Shanghai is good, better, because of the foreigner population?"

"Well, they're not all great. But for the most part, I think they're friendly people. At least I've never had any bad experiences with them."

"What experiences have you had?" asked the young man.

"Nothing special, you know, just day to day."

"Shu's husband is so afraid, he won't even go up to talk to them civilly," Bo laughed. "He doesn't know how to interact with them or make them feel at home."

"Why should I make them feel at home?" asked the young man. "They aren't at home. Their home is on the other side of the planet, that's where they'd feel at home, not here."

"Hey, see that?" Bo nodded discreetly to the foreign family a few tables away. Among them was a radiant blond-haired young woman. "How about that girl, huh? I wouldn't mind being introduced to her. If she can accept Chinese food, she can accept a Chinese man – and I'm a good cook, even in bed . . ." A smile crept across his face.

"That's repulsive, Bo," Shu reprimanded. "They look like a nice family. They're making an effort to eat our food and connect with our country."

"Go talk to her," said the young man. "She'll throw a cup of tea in your face. That could be the best thing you do tonight."

"You don't think she'll fall in love with me, sir?"

"You think just because she eats Chinese food that she will want to be with you?" asked the young man, his voice rising. "She might invite you to be her servant, her lackey. Her cook. Is that what you mean, Bo?"

Beside the blond woman was a handsome older man, obviously her companion, his arm around the back of her chair. She leaned into him to hear him speak, not taking her eyes off his face. The young man couldn't imagine a woman looking at him with such adoration and he let out a sigh, louder than he intended. Bo turned to stare.

"Look at that guy sitting right beside her. He's a handsome devil. Why, he could come over and sweep Shu here off her feet, steal her right from under your nose."

Although Bo had made his remark with a laugh, the joke fell flat, as though none of them could deny how handsome the foreign man was. The young man felt Shu shifting uncomfortably in her chair. He caught his breath as she placed her hand in his lap.

"That would never happen," she whispered.

"What about his big green eyes, Shu? What do you think is in his pants?"

"You're drunk, you idiot, stop it!" The young man placed both his hands on the table, as if he was going to stand up and charge at Bo's smirking face.

"What's wrong? Don't you like the colour green?" Bo winked. "I'm not afraid of you. Or of that white foreigner. We'll settle this once and for all." The young man watched as Bo hiccupped and got to his feet, staggering slightly.

He walked over to the foreign family. "Hello, friends," he called out. The young man, from where he sat beside Shu, cringed as he heard the servile tone in Bo's voice. He had never heard Bo speak in English, and the words sounded harsh and ugly.

The young man looked at the four foreigners, each dressed elegantly, with their clean faces, blond and brown hair. They looked uncomfortable. The young man wondered if such a thing had happened to them already on their trip in China. Maybe someone had stared at them, come up like Bo was doing now, even sat down beside them.

"How is food?" Bo asked, making a motion as if shovelling something into his mouth.

"Uh," said the handsome man, whom Bo was addressing, "fine, it's very good, thank you."

"Okay, okay." Bo broke into a grin, showing his discoloured teeth. "This restaurant very good. So good food." He made a circular motion indicating his stomach.

"Yes, we think so too."

"It my friend, birthday." Bo waved his arm in Shu's direction.

"Oh wonderful," said the man without enthusiasm.

The young man watched, both in horror and nervousness. The green-eyed foreign man found Shu in the crowd of Chinese faces and, seeing her beauty, raised his teacup. "Happy birthday," he said in a loud voice. The other foreigners at the table, including the beautiful blond, all waved. The young man felt the air moving as Shu waved back, giggling, but embarrassed.

The young man watched as Bo came back to the table. "You toad," Shu hissed. But she was trying to hide her laughter. "That was so obnoxious."

"See, I was right," Bo said. "That man wished Shu a happy birthday. So it wasn't a complete failure." Bo nudged Shu in the ribs. "Maybe next time he will sing the song for you and pop out of a birthday cake."

"That's enough," the young man said. "Let's go home."

"But I'm not tired. It's not even late." Shu placed a slender hand on her fiancé's sleeve.

"You guys go party without me." Bo waved his hand and belched loudly. "I'm a bit light-headed."

Outside, the friends parted, Bo going off on his own. The couple, the young man and Shu, began walking home. On the street, they passed by the entertainment district and Shu stopped. "Let's do something fun. I was born under the sign of the Rooster, remember?"

So the young man was often reminded. It meant that she was proud and liked to strut about, according to the astrologers.

Right on that street was a dance club. They were in the upscale One Hundred Happy Doors District, which was frequented by all types of people, from every country. There was a customer puller at the door, who usually targeted foreigners. But seeing Shu, he beckoned them inside.

"Come on, baby, we never go to these kinds of places. I want to try dancing."

The young man thought about what Bo had said. He didn't want Shu to think he was afraid of foreigners. He didn't want her to think he was so insecure that he couldn't take her to a dance club.

It was crowded, even in the hallways, on the stairwell that led upstairs to where people were dancing. The young man went to the toilet. "I'll go get some drinks at the bar," Shu said. "Come find me there."

The bathroom was cramped, filled with tall, muscular foreigners, many of whom busily fixed their hair in the mirror. They brushed past the young man as if he didn't exist. A stench of urine and booze blanketed everything.

At the bar he saw Shu, with her elbows on the counter. Two men were talking to her. She placed her hand on one of their thick, hairy arms, just for a moment. She seemed like a different person.

The young man approached her, feeling a surge of confidence and jealousy. *I'll grab her and just tell her we're leaving.*

When she saw him, she held out her hand. She pulled him close, kissing him. She introduced him to her two new acquaintances. The young man stood dumbly, stupefied by her reaction.

"This is Mark," Shu said, in Chinese. "He's a computer game designer. Cool, huh? The other one is Doug. He's a lawyer for an American company, from New York."

Then she introduced her fiancé. "This — my friend," she said. The young man didn't know much English, but he knew the word *friend*.

"Why did you call me 'friend'?" he argued in Chinese. "Why do you call me 'hubby' in Chinese, but 'friend' in English?"

"I said 'boy-friend,'" Shu said.

"So? Why 'boy-friend'? Why not 'hubby'?"

Shu laughed it off, giving no further answer.

Mark wasn't especially good-looking. In fact, Mark had thinning hair and a growing waist, probably in his forties. But Doug, the lawyer, resembled the green-eyed tourist from the restaurant, whom they had just seen. Doug had very clear, blue eyes. He was tall and handsome, probably in his thirties, with brown hair and a stubbly, chiselled jaw.

"Why don't you sit with us?" Doug said, directing his question to Shu.

The young man shook his head. But Shu was already walking away, leaving him behind.

Over her shoulder she shouted in English, "You — don't — mind, okay? Just — for — a — few — minute." She laughed, turning away before he could answer. He watched her continue speaking to the foreign men. "Practice make perfect! My English so good, right? I always practise, every time!" She winked at one of the men. Doug.

They squeezed through the crowd of bodies that were swaying and gyrating in the club, and sat down at a semicircular booth, looking out to the dance floor. Somehow Shu was seated between the two foreign men. Shu's fiancé was on the edge of the booth.

He watched as Shu talked. Because of the loud music, they leaned close to each other. She seemed to be curled up with Doug. The man had his arm around the back of her seat.

Shu finished a beer that wasn't hers. She leaned toward the young man, across the table. "Can you get some more of the drink?" she asked, in her accented English. She reached over and stuffed some cash into the young man's hand. Then she fell back into her chair before he could scold her.

Instead of yelling at her, he slid out of the booth. The bar was crowded. The young man waited behind five or six bodies. At last, the bartender grabbed the cash from his hand and thrust something onto the counter.

He felt almost relieved, hoping that Shu would pay attention to him now. But when he returned to the table, Shu wasn't there. The spot where she and Doug had been sitting was empty. Only Mark, the computer game designer, was present.

The young man sat quietly, not willing to address the foreigner. Finally, he couldn't stand it any longer. "Shu, where's she please?"

Mark yawned, patting his balding head. "She's on the dance floor. Why don't you go join her?" Mark slapped the young man on the back, in an exaggerated fashion, motioning to the mass of moving, rhythmic bodies.

She was dancing with Doug. They were so close together. Their bodies touched and pressed and moulded together.

He tried to move. But his body was wound so tight, he was immobile.

She came back, pulling Doug by the hand, through the crowd. Her face beamed and she seemed unapologetic.

Without looking at her fiancé, she took the drink from his hand – the drink she had sent him to get. She drank it in two gulps. She laughed and tickled him. "Don't be sore," she whispered in Chinese, "I'm only having fun, don't worry. Do you want me to sit with you?"

The young man was confused. Shu sat down with him on one side, Doug on the other side. She squeezed the young man naughtily, slipping her hand into his lap. She caressed him while Doug was right there and could see. "I love you, baby," she whispered into the young man's ear, in Chinese. "Just let me have some fun tonight, okay? It's my birthday."

She drank her fiancé's drink too. She was already drunk, but as she grew drunker, she became very quiet, very serene. Another round of beers came. She drank silently, listening to Doug shout across the table with Mark.

"I have to use the bathroom," Shu announced. She skirted over Doug's lap, without Doug getting up. As she passed, the young man saw her hand slip down. Her slender fingers pressed on the crotch of Doug's pants.

The young man sat, drinking his beer, ignoring his surroundings, not knowing what to do. The other two men stood up and left without a word.

When he came out of his stupor, Shu still wasn't at the table. There were people beside him. But he didn't recognize any of them, and they didn't look at him. Another couple in the booth were making out, kissing each other passionately, climbing over each other's bodies. He had never seen them before. He couldn't remember when Shu had left. The young man scrambled to his feet. He strained to look for her.

She was dancing in the middle of the floor – surrounded by people on all sides. She was dancing without a smile on her face. So many people were right beside her, so closely packed together that it was difficult to tell who was dancing with whom.

She was looking down and moving her body. She was looking down her shoulder, then down her other shoulder. She had her hands behind herself, touching somebody, touching another person's body. She was bathed in the music, in the darkness, in the strobe lights. Her face was serious, deadened even.

The young man pushed his way closer until he saw. Doug, the blue-eyed lawyer, was behind her. She was pressed with her bottom into him. They moved to a rhythm that the young man had practised with her naked in bed, at home.

He saw her slip her hand behind herself, behind her bottom, moving up to where Doug's crotch touched her.

The young man's face twitched. He pushed until he was near her.

"Where have you been?" she cried into his ear. She pulled him closer, without stopping her gyrating. She was closed in, between the two men. One larger, with his skin reflective in the flashing lights, and the other dark and small, unsure of himself and self-conscious.

"Don't," he said to her. He pulled her away from the other man. "I don't want you to do that. Please, come home with me now."

"Oh, you go, go out," she slurred. "I'll come later . . . half-hour more. Baby, wait for me outside. Just a half-hour." She kissed him on the mouth, and he tasted the sour alcohol.

The young man took the stairs down. He stood at a bar counter, absent-mindedly picking up an empty beer bottle. The hardness of bottle in his hand, and his anger, made him want to smash something. After what felt like a half-hour, he went back up. But when he scanned the crowd, he couldn't see anyone he recognized.

For the next few minutes, he stumbled up and down the stairs of the club, looking, muttering to himself, a wave of panic churning in his stomach.

He took out his mobile phone. His sweat glistened on its screen. If only he could turn back time to earlier in the night, to the silly dinner, that foreign family he had been so ridiculously afraid of. He dialed Shu's number. It rang and rang, but there was no answer.

He walked down a long hallway, where the music was only a gentle thump of beats. Outside the women's washroom, he thought he heard a familiar chime. He pushed the door open and found Mark inside, leaning against a sink, looking quite lethargic.

The chirpy ring of Shu's phone continued uninterrupted. "Where is Shu?" the young man croaked, his throat dry. He scanned the bathroom from one end to the other. At the far stall, he saw Shu's high heels jutting out from under the door. *She must be on her knees.*

The young man pushed the door of the unlocked stall ajar. Shu had taken the foreign man into her mouth. He knew it. He had always known.

"Hey, wait your turn," Mark said, with a grunt, holding out his arm, blocking him. "She did me already."

The young man couldn't understand the words, but it didn't matter. With one motion he pulled Shu backwards. He saw the man slide out like a long, thick, pink-purple snake. She tried to stand, tipsy on her feet, looking up at her fiancé.

The young man turned to face Doug, the blue-eyed foreigner, the lawyer from New York, whose pants were down around the ankles. Up until that point, the young man's anger had carried him. But seeing Doug exposed, he dropped his arms and just stared silently at the big fleshy thing between the white man's legs.

It took only a moment. Doug lashed out, swinging his hairy fist, hitting the young man square in the jaw and knocking him down.

Lying on the floor, the young man felt one of the club's bouncers lift him up by the armpits and half-drag him into the hallway. All the young man could do was groan.

Outside, the bouncer shoved him toward the street, where the young man tripped and fell again, coming to rest against an abandoned food stall. *This is as good a place to sleep as any*, he thought. Just as his eyelids began to close, he caught a glimpse of Shu. She stumbled on her high heels, waving in the young man's direction. The two men, one on either side of her, pulled her toward them, helped her into a car and followed in behind her.

10.
The Bicycle Thief

ONE

THEIRS WERE STOLEN, BUT MINE WAS NOT. WE HAD COME back from Inner Mongolia, on a weekend bus trip. Seventeen bicycles, which had been parked and locked in front of the guest house. They never found out who did it.

I had bought mine from a little bicycle repair shack, from an old, toothless man. Nobody else in our group had liked the look of him when we'd first passed by. They all continued walking. From the nice storefront shop, they purchased shiny new bicycles, ten speeds, with novelty horns fixed on the inner part of the handlebar.

"Don't be such a cheapskate," they had said, laughing. They ambled off, twenty of them, heckling and snapping their fingers in each other's faces. They jumped up and down in the dusty road.

I shrugged and lingered by the shack. The old man had me charmed the moment I saw him. He was soft-spoken and I had to get close to hear what he was saying.

He was a tiny man. Even when he was younger, he couldn't have been very large. He seemed like someone at the end of a long life, when they've been through a whole century of troubles. In the end they're more or less in the same shape as they were at the beginning: thin and hairless. But he looked indestructible, like the excess of his body had dried up, leaving only a wrinkly core.

He still had a little bit of grey hair on his spotty head. His face was severe looking, but not in any personal way. He didn't direct it toward you, it was just the way his face had been shaped over the years. He had a slight hunch in his back. But he didn't walk with a cane.

"You want to buy a bike?" he asked with surprise, when he finally understood my poor Chinese. He stood there, scratching his head, looking at me. He looked at the assorted junk that was around us.

All he had in the world, really, was a low tin shack with a hole for a window. There was just enough space inside for his cot. Outside, he had set up a small roof of corrugated metal to keep the rain and sun away. There were piles of broken bricks and buckets of old bicycle parts and tools: pumps, wrenches, tires, broken spokes and wheels. All in such frightful condition that any good shop would have thrown them out without thinking twice. All of this, his worldly possessions, could have been seized at any moment by the police. He had no permit to be a squatter there, by the side of the road.

I watched him for a little while, methodically hammering on a nut. He was trying to make it fit a bike that had been brought in to be fixed. The customers' bikes were locked up on one side, underneath the slanted roof. Some of these were shiny, expensive-looking things. Others were decrepit, like they had been pieced together with rubbish. The worst of these was a tiny red bike. The spine bar was lowered. You could dismount by moving your leg through the body of it, instead of swinging around the back.

"I'll take that one," I said, pointing to it.

Of course, he couldn't sell his customers' bikes. But I had a feeling that the red one could not possibly have an owner. It was completely unusable. The seat was crooked. The front wheel was warped. The tires were busted. The handlebar was bent. The handle brakes dangled from wires. It was rusty all over. It looked like a truck had backed over it several times.

"This thing?" He limped over to it. He looked back at me to see if he had heard me correctly. "You want to buy this thing?"

"Shoo deh. Yes, please, if it's for sale."

I spoke right to him, looking directly into his black, liquidy eyes. A slow, peculiar smile crept over his face. He reached into his pocket and produced a set of keys. He found the one he needed. There was a long chain lock, linking the bikes together through the wheels. He unlocked it, pulled the red bike out and set it in front of me. He let out a soft little chuckle and cleared his throat.

"It rides better than it looks." He straightened up to his full height and his voice assumed a serious, businesslike tone. "It just needs some work."

I tried to sit down on it, but the seat fell off.

"Not like that," the old man said. He stooped down and snatched the seat up in a flash, quicker than I could have moved. "Here, move out of the way, let me fix it." Nudging me forward, he slipped the seat back into its spot and deftly smacked it down in place. I was a klutz next to him. "There, now try," he said with his dry, hoarse low voice.

The handles were covered with dirt. Back then anything left alone in that city for a day would be covered with a thick layer of grime. When he saw that I was hesitant, he hobbled over. Using a black, sooty rag, he wiped down the handlebars. He wiped the seat for me. He cleaned the broken pipe that was keeping the rim from falling off. He wiped the tires. I protested that it was enough.

"Sihng, okay. Go on then, take it for a spin."

Very awkwardly, I pedalled the tortured bike a few yards, wobbling from side to side. The foot pedal gave way underneath my shoe. The old man came shuffling up behind me. He pointed to the ground.

"I can fix that," he said, a little embarrassed. "It'll only take a minute."

We brought the bike back under the roof of his shop.

"Howh, howh, that's fine. How much do you want for it?" I knew he could repair it so that it would be in good shape. A man like that has to know his trade, otherwise he starves to death. I pulled my shirt up to reveal a fanny pack, a battered green nylon one that I always took with me when I travelled. I unzipped the front pocket to take out my wallet.

He hummed and hawed, clearing his throat and stepping back. He put his hand on his hip. He scratched his head and stepped up to the bike. He shook it carefully, keeping a good grip on it, as if to show how sturdy it was.

"You know, it looks bad. But it's not a bad bike. It has a solid body. And there's no real permanent damage to it. You see, it's had a lot of owners, it's lasted a long time, that's how you know it's a good bike." He nodded his head to himself, as if in very deep thought. I didn't say anything. I nodded my head too and waited for him to decide. "Well, how about . . ." He paused. "How about ninety dollars, ninety kuai?"

It sounded like a perfectly reasonable price to me. But I wagged my head back and forth, with a frown on my face.

"You can have a lock, of course, a new lock for free," he added, as if he had forgotten. "I usually sell these for twenty kuai each. It comes with two keys." He took down some new bicycle locks that were hanging off to the side. He demonstrated how it opened. "What do you think?"

I nodded, taking my time, counting my money.

"Naturally," he said, with his businesslike air, "I'll fix up the bike for you. If you come back in an hour, I can straighten out the wheel. I'll give it the works. I'll put on new tires. You can use my tire pump here any time you want, no charge."

"What about the brakes?" The brakes were the most important, I figured. I wanted to stop every chance I had, to look at everything around me.

"Oh, the brakes, that's not a problem, I can get them in working condition for you. May wentee. That's a simple job."

"Do you have a basket? I'd like a basket on the front too, to carry my books."

"Sure, yes." He produced a lopsided metal basket, like a tiny cage to be attached above the front wheel, from the handlebars. "You can have this one. It's old, but it works fine. I'll put it on for you."

"Wonderful," I said, smiling. I put the money in his hand. "Tay howh lah. I'll be back tonight, or tomorrow to pick it up then."

I got back to our guest house before the others. I was lying in bed reading a book when I heard them outside parking their new bikes. I went out to take a look. They were still locking them up. They stood there, admiring them, honking their funny horns. They were cleaning them after the first ride, to keep them shiny.

"Not bad, very fancy," I said, coming down the steps. There were a few different styles. But they were all nice-looking.

"Aren't they though?" they congratulated each other.

There were two sisters in the group. One was nineteen and the other fourteen. We never succeeded in finding out where they had come from, only that they were something Asian, very dark-skinned and very pretty, from a wealthy family.

"Where's your bike, Danny?" the older one teased, whose name was Holly. "Did it break down when you were riding it back? Did you dump it in the river?"

"He probably crashed it into a tree," said Miander, the younger one.

Across from our guest house was a small stream that ran all around the campus. It was a river filled with luscious plants and lilies. In the summer, these strange tall red flowers bloomed and spread over the water like weeds. All along its embankment were stones, so that you could walk right up to the water's edge. How calming it would be to ride my bike along it, gazing at the reeds bending in the wind.

On the other side, opposite the hotel where we were staying, was an open stone terrace. The pagodas here had red-and-black intricately carved roofs. At night, along wooden walkways, people would sit and talk.

"I'm picking it up tomorrow," I told them.

"How much was it?" Holly, the older sister, asked.

I answered truthfully, not knowing whether I had been ripped off or not.

"Ninety ren min bee? Mine was two hundred and fifty," said one of the other students.

"Just wait till you see it," said Holly. "I bet it's a piece of junk."

Back in my hotel room, I lay in bed, thinking about my bike. My roommate Simon, a year younger than me, came in. I didn't know much about him, but he gave me a strange feeling. Perhaps we were too alike. We were both thin and wore eyeglasses, with short, cropped hair. He seemed, like me, detached from everyone else, somewhat of a loner, socially awkward. When we were in our room alone together, I would catch him staring at me.

"What's up?" I said, raising my eyebrow at him.

He frowned and shook his head whenever I looked in his direction. I commented on how he had bought a nice bike and asked him a bit about himself. He didn't answer any of my questions and wouldn't look at me. I excused myself to use the bathroom.

It was a nice hotel, modern and clean. The bathroom was spotless, the white tiles, the lighting, the mirror, the bathtub. Sitting on the toilet I noticed the vent near the bottom of the bathroom door.

I looked at the slats, angled so that I could only see down toward the carpet outside the bathroom door, in our room. I could see movement back and forth, the shadow of someone pacing. It went on and on, and I heard muttering. "Simon?" I called out. But there was no answer.

I liked the hotel, but with Simon in my room, it was somewhat uncomfortable. I went to the concierge, where there was a place to sit. It was a small building, built like a bunker, with a modest lobby, only a few round tables and chairs.

"What are you doing, drawing dirty pictures?" a voice asked. I twisted around in my chair. It was Holly.

"It's nothing," I said. "Just a poem."

"You're a poet?"

"Well, not really. I'd like to be. Want to read it?"

"Ugh, lame plus a million," she said. "God no."

"Okay." I shrugged. "Up to you."

"Wait. Give it to me." She took the paper, without sitting down, and glanced at it, pursing her lips. She let out a groan and tossed the paper back on the table in front of me.

"What's that?" she said, picking up a different wad of papers.

"Some stories I'm writing."

"Don't you have anything better to do?"

"Well, not really." I shuffled some of my other papers, hiding them out of sight. Our whole group had culture and language classes during the day, and I was about to start my calligraphy homework.

"You wrote this?" She cleared her throat and began reading from one of the papers: "'Our first kiss was in a twenty-four-hour Tim Hortons. She came back from the restroom and' blah blah blah."

Holly looked up from the paper with a frown, her shoulders sagging, heaving air out of her lungs like she had finished a marathon.

"Aren't you going to keep reading?" I said. "That's just two lines."

"More than enough." She handed the papers back to me. "Anyway, what are you doing sitting here? Why not work in your room?"

"My room? I don't know."
"How's Simon?"
"Who?"
"Your roommate," she said. "Simon."
"Oh, so-so, I guess."

After she left, I picked up the story she had read from and scanned the rest of the page:

> With her everything is different. Summer days, sun streaming through the window, both of us sleeping like dolls. Waking with her pressed up to me, I'm afraid of nothing.
>
> She falls asleep with a snap of the fingers. She sleeps with her hands behind her head, like she's lying in a hammock on a beach in Hawaii.
>
> I like winter the most. Watching her stomping her boots. In a blizzard, we trek two feet-deep miles through fresh snow.
>
> At home, exhausted, we fall dizzily on the carpet frozen and frostbitten, wriggle out of our clothes until we're shivering naked on the floor.

Later, I went out, walking off-campus.

At the campus gate, a guard stood at attention. Outside the gate, the surrounding area was bustling. Nearby were four different universities, their campuses all squished together. I found a strip mall with a little bookshop on the second floor called Book Worm. It was such a tiny shop. But books were piled to the ceiling. It reminded me of my favourite bookshop back home, in Toronto.

At dinner, we had to travel down the small road. Around the bend was a special dining hall reserved for us, with our own catering staff. Everybody had bikes to ride, except for me.

As I was walking the quiet road, they started passing me two, three at a time, whizzing by. Some slowed down and taunted me in good fun. They laughed and made jokes. Then they pedalled off in a fury, kicking up the dust and gravel in my face. The youngest of them was twelve or thirteen, mere kids. The oldest was twenty-one.

Holly came rushing past me, along with four others who were close to our age. They behaved just like the twelve-year-olds. I laughed at them as they tried popping wheelies and bunny-hops to show off on their bikes.

Holly slowed down and rode back around me. She made a wide turn, coming up from behind again. "You're going to be late for dinner," she said.

"Yah, you're going to be late for dinner, *loser*," echoed her younger sister. She had an unusual voice for a child – dry, sarcastic, incredibly snooty. She tossed her hair back.

"We're going to eat all the pork chops, then you'll be sorry."

"That's okay," I said, walking along at my unhurried pace, "I don't eat meat; I'm a vegetarian."

"Well, we'll eat all the vegetables then," Holly called out.

"Ew, I'm not eating vegetables," protested Miander. She sped off, laughing. Holly followed her, leaving me behind.

I walked on, past a dirty, grey area. They were doing construction by the bend. The road was bumpy, made up of large stone slabs poorly fitted together. My feet hurt.

After a little while, I was alone; I must have taken a wrong path. I couldn't find the dinner hall and I retraced my route. Then I heard someone on a bicycle. I heard the tread of tires on tiny pebbles.

"Danny?" said a voice. It was Holly.

"I'm over here," I said, coming out around a corner.

"What are you doing here?" Her face was tight, held together by suspicion.

"I got lost."

"Loser."

"Let me ride on the back of your bike."

"No, get away. You're too heavy."

She had a thin little figure. I knew that she would have trouble pedalling if I sat on the back.

"Get off then," I said. "It'll be easier for me to pedal you."

"What? Don't be sexist."

"I'm not being sexist," I said, holding up my hands in disbelief. She sat there frowning at me.

"If this is the thanks I get for giving you a ride, forget it," she puffed, blowing a wisp of hair out of her face. "*Sheesh.*"

I shrugged. "Fine, up to you." I sat down behind her. She had trouble even moving the pedal forward.

"You're too fat," she grunted.

"I told you."

"Get up and let me get some speed. You'll have to jump on."

"I'm not jumping on the back – look how small the seat is. It's not even a real seat."

"Quit whining. *I'm* the one who's doing all the work. *Sheesh.*" Without waiting for me to answer, she started pedalling forward. I had to skip quickly behind her and then hop on. I managed to land on the seat, and my momentum caused her to swerve to the side.

"Watch – what the hell!" she screamed.

But through a miracle we didn't crash. She jerked the handlebars back, and I nearly fell off. The road, with its large uneven slabs, was extremely rough. I had nothing to hold on to, except for her.

When we got to the dinner hall, I hopped off, and she locked up the bike. We went in through the double doors together.

"Did you do that on purpose?" she asked, giving me a mean, accusing look.

"What? What on purpose?"

"You know what, touching me."

"I held onto you because I was about to fall."

She stared at me with a pout, as if unable to decide whether I was telling the truth. "Fine, whatever." She spun around, leaving me behind. "If it's not consensual, it's assault."

We were late when we sat down for our meal. The food was untouched as it was every night. The children ate a few bites from each of the dozen or so dishes. Afterward the wait staff wheeled out garbage tubs and dumped piles of food. Two huge tables' worth, entire lobsters and seafood, the best and carefully roasted meat, and exquisitely prepared vegetables.

"That's such a waste," I said, only to elicit laughter and shrugs.

The next day I went to pick up my bike.

Some of them didn't have anything to do, so they came out for a ride. About fifteen of them, like stragglers tagging behind and in front of me. They rode on the grass, on the bank of the river, and tried to do wheelies.

"I can't wait to see this piece of crap you bought," said Miander, in her dry, irresistible voice. They wore only expensive designer clothes, tight-fitting fashions. They looked like twins. Both with the same thin figure and same dark, bewitching face. Except that Holly was taller.

Having all those people there made me nervous. Wouldn't it be embarrassing if the shack was gone? Maybe the old man had packed up his whole business and moved across the city so that he could keep what I had paid for already.

But he was still there, of course. Right over a tiny drawbridge, down the way. Over a narrow section of the river, which curved and split and curved again. He was sitting, just like the day before, under the tin roof, on a little folding stool. He had an odd-shaped tool in his hand. A different bicycle was propped up, upside down in front of him, and he was wearing big spectacles that I hadn't seen the day before.

When he saw me, he put his work down. He stood up and shuffled away to fetch my red bike. He brought it out into the open, in front of us. Under the sun, it was very hot.

"Here you go," he said, nodding his head.

It looked in much better shape than the day before. I could see that in a glance. Everything looked in order. The paint was still scratched up, but somehow it didn't look so rusty.

There was even a handbell that he had put on for me. A cheap little thing, but an extra doodad nevertheless. I only needed streamers off the handlebars now. I tested the brakes and they worked just fine.

"Are these your classmates?" He looked at the other children. We must have looked like a funny bunch because of the variation in our age. "Where are you from?" We answered generally, without being too specific, to avoid confusion. He was only making conversation, however, because he was professionally interested in their fancy bikes. "Where did you get those?" he asked, unable to hide his curiosity. He went up and examined their spanking new bikes.

"Just down the street," Miander answered. "Over at the shop there."

He crouched down and checked out her wheels. He shook his head. I couldn't tell if it was because he was disappointed. And of course he asked them how much they had paid.

He nodded his head, adjusting his flimsy spectacles. "It must be good business for you," I said, "if the shop sells so many bikes, the customers will bring them to you to get them fixed."

"Oh no. I am sure the shop fixes them for free, for their customers. That's how it works."

"It's true. That's what the man who sold them to us said," Holly confirmed.

She spoke in English. She and her sister refused to speak the local language, which they knew already. But why they refused, I could not get them to explain – it was the usual answer: just because.

The old toothless man then asked how long we were staying in the city.

"For three months," someone in our group answered, one of the younger kids. "Four," said another.

"But what will you do with the bikes when you leave?"

"We can sell them back to the store for half price. That's what the salesman said."

The old man nodded his head. I was staying on for longer than the rest of them, so I would keep my bike. When I had made sure everything was in order, I thanked him, we all did, and then we went off to the guest house.

On the way back, the right pedal fell off as I was riding it.

"HAHAHAHAHA!" Miander, who was riding behind me, shouted, crashing her bike in her fit of laughter.

I had to get off the bike and look at why it had fallen off. I couldn't tell, of course. I didn't know the first thing about bikes. The nut had come loose somehow. That was all I could see. The threads were worn down. I tried to slip the shaft of the pedal back onto its proper place. But it wouldn't stay put.

"I'll walk back to the shop with you," said Holly.

"Are you sure?"

"Why not?" She raised her eyebrows, looking at me directly.

"Holly loves Danny," sang Miander, "Holly loves Danny. Holly and Danny, sitting in a tree, K-I-S-S-I-N-G, first comes love, then comes marriage, then comes baby in the baby carriage."

We went off, the two of us together, alone. I pushed my bicycle on my right side, with the detached pedal in the basket. Holly followed with her bike, to my left.

We walked in silence for a little while, with the sound of the pebbles and the crunching of the dirt path underfoot.

"You're really strange, you know that?" she said.

"I am? What do you mean?"

"I don't know, you're just – strange."

"Why?"

"Well, why did you buy such a crummy bike?"

"It's not a crummy bike. It's a wonderful bike."

"I don't know why you say that. The pedal just fell off it," she said, with a painful grin.

"That's what you have to put up with, if you want a great bike. It's a trade-off," I said.

"What do you mean 'trade-off'? It *fell* off." I didn't know what I could say, except grunt. "So, what are you doing here?" She changed the subject in my silence.

"I'm going to pick up my bike."

"No, I mean, what are you doing *here*, in this *country*. Kevin says you're staying here after the camp is over. Is that part of your stupid 'being a poet' idea?"

"No, it's got nothing to do with that. I don't know why, really."

"What, you're just bumming around? You don't have a reason? Don't you think you should go home, get a job? What do your parents think?"

"Yeah, maybe. I wanted to come see what it was like," I said. "Also, I got kicked out of school last year."

"You did? You loser. What did you do, hit on your teacher?"

"I plagiarized an essay."

"I thought you liked writing."

"I do," I said.

"Then why'd you cheat?"

"I don't know. I was going through a rough breakup at the time. I wasn't thinking."

"Wow, you really are pathetic. What was she like?"

"Who?"

"The girl who dumped you."

"She was special."

"Okay, I get it. You got your heart broken, then you got kicked out of school for cheating, so you came here to this shithole to become a poet. You really are a joke."

I didn't know. Maybe Holly was right. I felt like a failure, and my life hadn't even started.

TWO

A year earlier, I was studying for a degree, back in Canada. There were sofa chairs behind me, comfortable red ones, and students chatting with each other. To one side was a broken, clunky piano, where someone was banging out a tune. I walked over to the computer terminals and opened up my email account. There it was, a letter from the department chair. The sentence jumped out at me:

This is to inform you that you are being investigated for an academic offence.

I had submitted the same essay to two different courses. In other words, I had tried to get double credit for the same work.

Submitting the same essay to save time and work seemed like a no-brainer. For the second submission, I fixed it up and changed the title to make it more relevant to the topic, of course. I wanted good marks, after all. Naive, but that was my nature.

Afterward, I tried to explain. It was hopeless though. All I could do was get a doctor's note. I went to the school's medical clinic where I began to panic, and then passed out on the floor of the waiting area.

I explained my impending expulsion to the doctor who treated me that day. "I've been so emotional," I said. "I haven't been thinking clearly. Maybe the professors will understand and be more forgiving." The doctor was sympathetic and wrote a note on my behalf. But in the end, it made no difference.

"Why'd you change the title?" the professors asked. "You were trying to hide what you were doing, weren't you?"

I hung my head guiltily. I was on a scholarship, so it was equivalent to stealing money. I was a thief, a cheat, a liar, a fraud. The feelings stuck with me. Only long after, when my past had hardened into an impenetrable rock, I thought about it in racial terms. Three white male professors – experts on Oriental histories, no less – their stony, dignified faces, and me with my sweaty palms, my black hair, dark and sullen body. The power they had, and the lack of power I had, was undeniable. If they saw beyond my face and last name, they never let on. My regard for them, for their prestige, kept me from questioning their authority and my shame.

Passing by an office door, I had once overheard a couple of grey-haired scholars conversing.

"You'd think a proper bibliography wasn't too much to ask for."

"Forget the bibliography. All I want is a citation."

"How do they manage to get this far?"

"On sampans, I presume."

The words had lingered in my brain, but I hadn't pieced it together. Who had they been speaking about? Now I understood. What was I but one among hundreds, thousands of Chinese exchange students, who had come here, for reasons of their own, to study humanities and arts?

"Have you ever been caught cheating before?" My interrogators put the same questions to me over and over. Maybe I was too young to know how to defend myself. I didn't raise my voice. All I did was mumble feebly and stutter. I was so nervous and confused, I called them by their first names. After two meetings, the professors wouldn't let me into their office. They must have been embarrassed of me, like I was some wild, uncivilized savage that reminded them of the vast divide between them, in their book-lined offices, and me, begging to be allowed to stay.

I had met her on a Greyhound headed out of Vancouver to a small town. I was playing with a puzzle, something like a brain teaser, sitting across the aisle from her. She sat cross-legged facing the window, with earphones on, looking out into the dark passing night. She had come from a Radiohead concert, as I later learned. When she saw that I had solved the puzzle, she gave me a thumbs-up, grinning. She had such a smile, such a face. I could have seen her for five seconds, and I would have remembered her for the rest of my life.

I had downloaded some pornography, something she had forbidden me to do. I don't know how she found out, but when I met her one evening at the SkyTrain, she was furious. We were on the platform and she ran out of the station, screaming. Someone saw me chasing her and called the police. The next thing I knew, a dozen police officers had me on the ground.

They interviewed us separately. It started to drizzle. They took her under the shelter of the station, putting a blanket over her shoulders, while I knelt down, officers around me, hands on their holsters. While talking to the officers, someone stole our bags, left on the sidewalk, and everything inside them – laptops, wallets, phones.

"You came to Vancouver together?" they asked.

"Yes, yes." Like always, nobody believed me.

"Are you on drugs?"

"No, I'm not."

They frisked me. I was a graduate student and had never touched a recreational drug in my life. Now there I was, my arms handcuffed behind my back, wet and shivering. They took everything out of my pockets.

They didn't ask her that question, or search her, of course. She loved doing drugs. Speed, ecstasy, coke, psilocybin mushrooms – anything she could get her hands on, including sniffing videotape cleaner fluid, which she once raved about. She smoked a few packs of cigarettes a week, drank anything and fantasized about doing heroin. She was a high school dropout and also a formally trained dancer who could have turned professional. Whenever we walked by music on the street, she would break into a dance, each time something new and mesmerizing.

"What did you tell them?" I asked her afterward.

"I told them that you watch porn, and I hate it."

Neither one of us knew how to fix things. We didn't know enough, we weren't old enough to know to apologize to each other, to forgive each other. We were too dumb, too inexperienced to figure out our lives, even though we loved each other.

It was in Vancouver, this city by the ocean, where I last saw her. I still remembered the way she waved. I got into a car and watched her on the sidewalk, in a strapless, pink-and-yellow minidress, doing a dance. We planned on being together after I came back from a trip. But when I returned, someone else – a young man who had once loved her – had died.

"I told him I was going back to you," she said, "and he committed suicide."

At his funeral, she promised his dead body, still and pale in the coffin, that she wouldn't get back together with me. And that was it.

THREE

Our group took trips outside the city. One weekend we went to Inner Mongolia. We took shade in huts and rode horses. We stayed in a nice hotel, at the end of a long, dark street. At night, I went out for a walk by myself.

Passing by a shop, I spotted a mature-looking woman, sitting in a skirt, her legs crossed.

"Where are you going?" she asked.

"Nowhere."

"Come sit with me."

"Okay," I said. There was another woman in the shop. I thought it was strange that they were sitting there on the sofa. A guy with a pot-belly showed up, sitting across from me.

"Where are you from? What are you doing?"

I couldn't understand their language. I didn't know where I was, or what they wanted to talk about. They laughed, and I laughed too. They seemed like such nice people.

"You – two – sisters?" I said. I got the hint that that's what she was telling me.

"Yes, yes, my sister." They nodded. "Come upstairs with us."

"Upstairs?" I shook my head. "I can't, no, I'm staying at the hotel. I'm from Canada," I said. "Jia-na-da."

"Ca-na-da? He says he's from Canada. Ha! Come upstairs, Canada Boy. You'll have a fun time."

I pointed up at the ceiling and they nodded. From their persistence, I figured they wanted to sell me something. "No, I don't have much money with me."

"You say you're from Canada? On vacation with no money? Turn your pockets out and I'll believe you." A woman made a motion to my pants.

"Like this?" I pulled the fabric of my pockets inside out, revealing wads of dirty tissue, which I had used during the day to wipe my nose. Little crumpled balls drifted to the floor.

"He's telling the truth, he's got no money, no friends, no family. Why else would he be here alone?"

They lost interest in me and went on talking among themselves. I listened for a while, but I couldn't understand. Eventually, I went back to the hotel and played the piano in the lobby for a while.

After the trip, in my room on-campus, I got more and more nervous. One morning I woke up with Simon standing next to me. He was whispering and holding his bible a few inches above my face. I was so surprised I nearly fell out of bed. Whenever I went to the bathroom, he would come over and pace outside the door, reciting some mumbo-jumbo.

"Simon? I can see your feet, through the vent." If I spoke to him enough, he would go back to his bed.

Maybe it was a mistake, but I told Holly when she asked me about him one day. "Simon's my half-brother," she said.

"Oh, okay, that's funny."

"He's a bit strange, but he's very smart. He's studying at Oxford."

Later that day, I was walking by the hotel lobby when Simon spotted me. He rushed over and grabbed my sleeve. "I know you've been talking about me." He held his fist up to my face. "You're lucky we're not at home, or else I'd punch your lights out."

I didn't know where 'home' was, but I was sufficiently scared.

"You can sleep on the floor of our room," my friend Kevin offered. "I don't mind."

Kevin and Jon shared a room. They lay on the bed, watching the TV at full volume late at night. Kevin would make snappy comments every minute about whatever program they were watching. I couldn't sleep.

There was someone in our group, a young woman named Violet, who lived in a room alone and had a spare bed. "Want to take the extra bed?" she asked. I didn't know anything about her, but she spoke English and seemed to be friends with Holly.

"I don't think that's a good idea," I said. "Isn't that like, inappropriate?"

"What's inappropriate about it? There are two twin beds and they're like, five feet apart."

I spent that night in her room. The evening passed uneventfully, but sometime at night I heard a voice.

"Are you awake?"

"Yeah, why."

"Want to talk a bit?"

"About what?"

"I don't know. Sit over here, I can barely hear you."

I got out of bed and sat down next to her. The next thing I knew, I was lying down and had an arm around her. It was awkward, and a minute later I got out of the bed.

"Sorry, I'm really sorry about that."

"Why?"

"Nothing, it just doesn't feel right."

"Okay." She turned her back to me, and we went back to sleep. The next morning, the monitor stopped me in the hall.

"What's this about you changing rooms?" he asked, accusingly. "You need to sleep in your assigned room, with your flatmate. Your flatmate is Simon. Is there any problem with him?"

"No, it's fine." I didn't tell him I was worried Simon would lop off my head in the middle of the night. It didn't matter anyway. If that happened, I'd probably be happy.

* * *

Our group took a day trip to Wangfujing, the famous pedestrian street. We saw gigantic, skewered insects, roasted and ready to eat: millipedes, grasshoppers, scorpions, all the size of my forearm. On the way back, getting off the bus, Kevin joked with Jon. Jon had bought something and was keeping it hidden in his backpack.

"What'd you buy?" I asked.

"Nothing, I'll tell you later." Jon turned his head and winked in my direction.

"Shhh, not so loud," Kevin whispered.

"What? Did you buy condoms?" I said in a voice loud enough for everyone to hear.

"Oh my god." Jon ducked his head down.

"Who are they for? What are you going to do with them?"

We all went out that night to Sanlitun, a bar district, popular and unregulated. Years later I visited the same district after the Olympics and the entire place was gone. There wasn't a trace of it left. It was all enormous, glass and steel buildings as far as the eye could see.

There were so many sex workers on that street, every ten feet someone stopped me. At length we found the disco we wanted to visit. It was Violet's birthday, and before 7:00 p.m., she was so drunk she couldn't stand. They all went into the club, but I took Violet home, to the hotel, and brought her to her room.

That night, I went out on my own. I walked out of the lobby, down the steps. My bike was still on the rack, the only one left after the theft. The only thing missing was the little fabric seat protector I had purchased for an extra five yuan.

Riding off-campus, I thought about all the places my bike had probably been, with all its owners. A bike like that had probably been through five owners. Perhaps more than five owners. It knew the city. It was like owning a part of the city.

I couldn't go very fast. But it was enjoyable cruising around the empty roads. I managed to get outside the campus walls and saw the wide-open streets. There were tired, dirty men sleeping out in the open. They had little beds set up between the inner road and the main road. They looked so peaceful under the artificial yellow brightness of the street lamps. I wondered how they could seem so content.

The brake on the front tire of my bike spun out, and when I pressed down, it wouldn't engage. But it didn't bother me. I never did bother to get it fixed. I just left it like that.

I found an alleyway, with people playing mah-jong, the traditional game with green-and-white tiles. Old men and women sitting at low tables, on footstools. Table after table clacking away. Then there were people playing at cards – just ordinary, plastic playing cards.

I rode to the end of the alley. It was so dark I couldn't see anything, I could only smell something foul. Turning around, I lowered my foot for balance.

I don't know what I stepped in, but my sock and shoe and foot were soaked.

Coming out of the alley, near midnight, I saw a tiny convenience stand. It looked terribly rundown. There were the usual smokes, drinks, Popsicles in dirt-smeared freezers. For sale were shoes too, white ones with blue-and-red racing stripes down the sides, made of cheap fabric. I threw away mine and bought those, brand-new, with shoelaces. I wore them without socks. They were perfect and very comfortable. For the rest of the time I lived in that city I bought that shoe, over and over again.

FOUR

The two sisters still puzzled me. "Where do your parents live?" I asked Miander one evening.

"I don't know." She shrugged.

That was as much information as I ever got out of her. On our day trips we took the chartered bus about the city. Kevin, whom

I thought was their cousin, sat near the back with me. "What the heck is up with your two cousins?" I asked him.

"They aren't my cousins."

"Do you know anything about them?"

"Their parents own the MTR, that's all I know."

"What's that?"

"The Hong Kong subway company."

The preposterousness of his claim left me breathless. Kevin's own family was the majority stakeholder of a major fashion group, Lane Crawford, so it wasn't entirely unbelievable. But just the thought that a family could own a whole subway system made my head spin.

Late the next morning, planning to spend the day by myself, I started out across campus, riding my bike. I wanted to see the nearby computer city complex, supposedly an immense network of buildings that sold electronics.

Passing the sports yard on campus, I dismounted and walked my bicycle. A young woman stopped me, holding out her phone. She was a head shorter than me, with thick horn-rimmed eyeglasses, short black hair to her shoulders and wearing old-fashioned clothes.

"Will you take a photo of me?" She posed with her fingers up in a *V*. I took a few snapshots. "Thanks," she said.

"You're welcome." I passed her camera back to her. "Hey, do you know where Electronics City is?"

She pointed in the direction I had been walking. "It isn't too far. What are you buying there?"

"An e-dictionary. Ever seen one of those?"

"Sure, I have one right here. Want to take a look?" We sat down on the edge of the field and she rifled through the objects in her enormous purse.

"This is great for learning English." She took out a handheld device. A few years later, with the advent of smartphone software, apps would replace these devices. But at the time they seemed to me indispensable. "Do you need some help picking a dictionary? I can come with you."

"Are you sure? It'll probably take the whole day."

"I've been in my room the entire week studying. I need a break."

I locked up my bicycle and we walked off-campus, the rest of the distance, until we reached the looming set of towers, the black blocky buildings.

"Phoenix and Dragon City." She swept her hand against the haze. We were in one of the best-known areas in Beijing, where everyone went to buy electric gizmos.

We went into one of the towers, full of densely packed stalls, cluttered with gadgetry. There were dozens of dictionaries to choose from. But making the choice was easier than I had thought. "I can't afford any of these," I said. The models were all above a thousand kuai.

"How much was yours?" I asked.

She shrugged her shoulders. "I didn't buy it. It was a gift from a friend."

"What's the cheapest one you have?" I asked the salesperson. I finally found one within my budget, a flimsy one with a plastic blue cover. "This is perfect. I'll take this one."

"You should see how it works first," the young woman said.

"They'll just try to upsell me."

The clerk patiently showed me the functions. "Do you want something with more options? I have a nicer model, only two hundred kuai more."

"No. I'll take this one."

I didn't want to stay in that busy place for too long. We came back outside, the late afternoon sun still bright and hot in the sky.

"Where've you been all day?" Simon, my roommate, asked as I entered our room.

"Nothing, just went for a walk."

He stood glaring at me. "You missed lunch."

"Yeah, because I wasn't here."

"If you miss lunch, you have to put your name on the sign-out sheet so everyone knows."

"Okay." I hadn't even known about the existence of a sign-out sheet.

He went out of the room, slamming the door behind him. A moment later, there was a knock.

"Come in," I said, from the bed.

"Danny?" I heard a female voice, Holly's. "What the hell are you doing?"

"What? Nothing," I said.

"Don't slam the door."

She lived in the room beside us, with her sister. "Yeah, Danny," came Miander's voice. "Don't slam the door, you douche."

"That wasn't me. That was Simon."

"Oh?" said Holly. "How's he doing?"

"Tell him to stop waking me up. This morning when I opened my eyes, he was holding a bible over my head. It scared the hell out of me." With Holly there, I didn't want to let the opportunity slip by. "Are you busy now? Want to go downstairs and walk around the pond?"

"Why?"

"I want to talk to you about something."

"About what?"

"I'll tell you in a bit. Let me use the bathroom first. I'll knock on your door."

In my bathroom I splashed water on my face. She was so mean to me, I couldn't say why I liked her. Maybe she could see how terrible I was inside, and that was why she was so mean. Maybe that was what I wanted, for someone to really see the real, awful me, so that I could know myself, and finally understand why I had made such inexplicable decisions. Maybe she would have the answer.

I didn't bother towelling off, and with my hair dripping and water still on my face, I knocked on her door.

"Why's your face wet?"

"Nothing, it's just water."

Downstairs by the pond, overgrown with lilies, we walked around. The channels were full of murky water and insects, vines twisting and creeping up onto the path, and fish silently below the surface.

"Holly, what do you think you'll do after the term is over?" She shrugged, and like her sister, had no answer for me. "Jon said you're planning to go to New York. Is that true?"

"Maybe, I don't know."

We were baking underneath the sun. All around us cicadas shrilled in the trees. In the shade of a carousel, we sat down on a bench in the pavilion. A handful of old ladies were doing a square-dance class. Two men sat on a ledge over the water, with fishing poles.

"Too many mosquitoes," she said, waving the air around her slender legs. "Why did you want to come out here? What did you want to talk about? It's so hot, it's gross." I didn't tell her it was the only way to have some privacy with her, away from her terrible little sister. I shifted a bit closer and put my hand near hers.

"What are you doing?"

"Nothing."

"Are you trying to hold my hand?" Her shocked voice hurt me. She stood up awkwardly and walked back. I hurried after her, trying to smooth things over by commenting on the hot weather, but it didn't help much. By the time we reached the hotel where we lived, almost hidden among trees, she still hadn't said a word. She walked through the glass front doors without looking behind her, and left me alone on the street outside.

11.
The Brothers

IN GANSU, THE DRIEST PART OF CHINA, TWO BROTHERS shared everything, including a name. All they owned was a tiny thatched hut, a broken television and two acres of arid, unfarmable land.

Older Liu, when he turned twenty-two, decided that it was time to marry. But he was too poor and he could not afford to keep a wife.

To him, a wife meant someone who would cook and clean. He wanted to know the feeling of having someone take orders from him. It was very much like getting a maid, or a house servant, except you only had to feed her instead of pay her.

The other thing was that he had recently noticed a pretty young woman, a girl, hardly of age.

Of course, he had seen her as a child. But in the past year or two, she had developed into a woman. Her name was Jade, and she was the youngest daughter of the Hsia family, which was even poorer than the two brothers. Her face was a pleasing, clear white with pink cheeks. Her eyes were big and round and black, and she had a small pouty mouth. She was thin and young, but large bosomed already. Older Liu found this combination very attractive.

It was uncommon, but not unheard of, that relatives, such as cousins, or brothers, should share a wife, because of financial reasons. It made sense, he reasoned, because the wife really had not that much to do, staying home all day. And having the responsibility of taking care of two husbands would better ensure that her time was spent properly, and not diverted to unhealthy interests.

One day Jade was walking by him and Older Liu stopped and told her he planned to marry her.

"Sho du," he said. "It will not be long before we are married, maybe two or three months. Do you think that is good?"

She was only sixteen, but in the poor villages, she was already regarded as a woman, as someone who had to begin to earn her own keep or to marry out of the family to relieve her parents of the daughterly financial burden.

She did not especially like Older Liu, however. He was gangly-looking, but not tall and skinny. He was big boned, but not fat. His legs seemed to be bulbous and large, and his arms were strangely grown, and dangled too far down, hanging almost to his knees. He had thinning hair already, and a long, hooked nose, and his skin was not very pleasant.

What Jade really wanted was to be independent, to go to the coast, or see a big city like Chongqing, or Shenzhen. She often talked to her sisters about this. "I want to travel from Gobi to Hainan, and of course visit Beijing. Imagine all the magnificent things I'd see."

From early in her childhood, she shared a room off the kitchen with her older sisters, while her little brother had his own room, close to the front of the house. They loved her and let her plaster the walls with old posters of the many tourist sites across the country. Jade's favourites were "Miracle of Yellow Mountain," "Beauty of Great Guilin," "Ink Painting-like Scenery of Xiapu, Fujian," "Sanya Island Beach Paradise," "Window of the World in Shenzhen," "Exotic Jiangsu Fan Gong Palace," "Xi'an City Splendid Great Wall" and "Tibet Potala Palace." There was hardly enough space on her walls.

The posters had another purpose as well, which was to keep the mud walls from flaking off. Jade, lying on her makeshift wood board bed, often woke with dried mud on her face, which had fallen from the ceiling or the walls. At night, she feared that the ceiling would cave in, that she would be buried alive. The idea of slabs of mud falling on her, closing her off from the world and blotting out the night sky, made her skin crawl with shivers before she fell asleep each evening.

Like everyone else in the village, her family was poor. It wasn't that she looked down on hardship or her family's poverty, but she didn't want to be stuck there in the village until she died. She knew she was meant to stay, and this made her frustrated and restless. She often wanted to try new things, even in the village, like eating a new kind of food, or talking to any new stranger. But there was only one road in and one road out, and it was lined with ditches filled with water that stank in the heat. There was never anything new, not food, not even a person.

At home, growing up, she helped her mother and father with the chores, doing what she could. Meanwhile her older sisters left for the big cities on the coast to look for jobs, husbands and money. The family needed money to send Jade's little brother to school, so it was a burden on the daughters, who dropped out and went to work at factories or massage parlours, sending most of their pay back home.

Jade stayed at home to care for her parents and little brother. The parents wished her to marry while she was young and could get a good bride price, which would be saved and then used when her younger brother wanted a wife. That was how the world worked. The daughters were yaoqianshu, a money tree.

As things were, Jade knew of Older Liu, even before he had tried to arrange their marriage. Because she had always known Older Liu's younger brother, Younger Liu, who was just seventeen.

* * *

Younger Liu was handsomer than his older brother. Which was to say, he was not as unattractive. He had a regular nose and face, without deformity, a modest jawline and a muscular torso. In short, he looked his age, a young man – whereas Older Liu looked already like an elderly one.

Younger Liu was happier too. When he and Jade played as children, she had felt pleased with herself, and it was easy to forget their poverty. Younger Liu made all sorts of games that they could play. Their favourite was to make-believe that he was a boar, a character from a famous book, Eight Precepts Pig from *Journey to the West*. He would wear a paper cup over his nose, tie leaves to his ears and use a curved branch around his waist for a tail. She would be Pigsy's wife, cloaked in a red cloth taken from her mother's closet, and ride on his back, one leg on either side. Astride like this, she would pinch his flanks and laugh uncontrollably as he trotted and kicked his hind legs up. His squealing and grunting made her flush with delight.

As a child, Jade told him about her dreams of travel. "Can you take me on a trip one day, Mr. Pigsy? How about if I ride you to Lhasa?" she suggested. "Or take me to visit the Terracotta Army in Xi'an. I wonder how they eat." In her childish mind, the statues were real living people made of dirt and stone who lived in mud houses, just like hers.

But they were grown up now. She had not thought seriously of marriage before, and that Older Liu should propose now frightened her. She wondered about Younger Liu, and what it would be like to be his sister. And she felt sad that it was Older Liu who had asked, and not his brother.

Younger Liu of course saw her new beauty also. Since she had grown up, he both wanted to see her and avoid her. Each time their paths crossed, he became short of breath and his heart pounded. He held his straw hat in front of his brown, unwashed trousers, to cover himself.

"Your brother has asked me to marry him," she said to Younger Liu, when she saw him in the road in front of her family home.

"And what will you say?"

"Well, I will have to marry him."

When Younger Liu left, Jade went into her bedroom and cried. But she could not be a burden on her parents any longer.

Younger Liu did not intercede. He felt that, if it was his older brother's wish, he could not oppose it. But, sitting on his cot, he hunched his shoulders and let his head sag, tears dropping to his lap. It was not until the next week, when his older brother sat down with him, that his mood changed. He saw that Older Liu, far from being elated, was upset and confused.

"Let me be honest with you," Older Liu said. "I am in a difficulty." And Older Liu explained that he had proposed to Jade.

"She's a beautiful girl, a woman now. But I am too poor to take care of her alone. Younger brother," he said, pausing, "do you plan on getting married too? What would you say if we – if we shared her? She could take care of both of us. It would be easier on everyone."

Younger Liu nodded his head, but he did not betray his own happiness. He frowned even, pretending to be considering it carefully. For a few moments he did not say anything, except to grunt, as he often did, to indicate understanding.

"Yes," he said finally, "I think it is okay. Let us talk to Jade and see what she thinks."

"You talk to her, younger brother. You were always closer friends with her. Tell her it is my decision, if she does not object. Tell her we will share her, and that way she will be better taken care of."

When Younger Liu went to see Jade the following night, he explained to her all that Older Liu had said.

"But what does that mean to share?" she asked.

"Well" – Younger Liu hesitated, not knowing how to reply – "it just means that you will help out both of us, when we need it. I thought your second elder cousin married this way too, didn't she?"

And it was true – Jade had a relation in the neighbouring village who had done the same thing.

"I don't know. But I am happy anyway, if it means we can be together."

So, they were married, Older Liu and Jade. It was in a small village, and she was of age, and among the locals nobody objected. And because it was not legally permissible for the brothers to share a wife, the additional marriage was done in a quiet manner, involving a simple ceremony and no witnesses. In the privacy of their home, Younger Liu prostrated himself, knocking his head on the floor before Older Liu and Jade, who sat in wooden chairs. After a moment, he wobbled to his feet and took a teapot in his hands. Older Liu and Jade held out their saucers and cups, and Younger Liu poured them tea. Finally, he bowed again to each of them, and begged for their forgiveness.

The brothers lived in the same hut. It had only three rooms. The brothers divided it up so that they each could sleep separately. They added a little extension, an extra room, so that Jade could have a place to put up her travel posters and arrange her clothes.

The Liu brothers were very pleased with the situation. They felt that their lives were much better with the presence of Jade, whose young, bright face made them happier. She missed her parents, but since they lived in the same village, she wasn't too heartbroken. She wanted to make a good life out of what she had – for herself, and for her sisters and parents. So she was a very good attendant to the Lius, sweeping the floors, preparing the meals, waking up early to make sure that everything was ready for the day to go smoothly.

They did not say specifically to her what else her responsibilities entailed. But on the first night Older Liu asked her to sleep in his bedroom, and on the second night Younger Liu did the same, and so on and so on, so that she alternated brothers each night. This seemed to satisfy the both of them, even though they never discussed it.

When they sat down to breakfast or lunch or dinner, they only spoke pleasantly about other things: the land, food, practical issues. No hint was made that she was sleeping with both of them, even though all three of them knew. The brothers did not seem to think too much about it.

But Jade, during her long days at home, wondered.

At first, she did not like it. She only wanted to pleasure one man, to give and devote herself to one man entirely. That was, after all, how she had always imagined marriage.

But over the course of that first month, she slowly saw that it was livable and fine, perhaps even better. Because they were brothers, it was her duty to make them both happy, since they had agreed upon this situation. She found herself alternating nightly between two different beds, with two different men. *It was a new kind of double happiness*, she thought to herself, *a double double happiness*. And this seemed reasonable.

Older Liu lay in bed when she came into his room. He waved his hand for her to close the door, even though she was already closing it. Then she walked over, silently, to the little poor dresser, and sat down on a round stool, combing her hair. She would sit there, politely pretending not to notice anything else.

When she walked over to the bed, four or five minutes later, she would slip under the covers. Older Liu's sleeping pants were always loosened, and drawn down, and he would be hard, a little hairy brown thing, which pointed straight up toward his belly button. She would slide on top of him, straddling him around the waist, and she would bend down to cover his mouth with hers, and kiss him long and lovingly, with her open mouth, letting him feel the inside of her mouth with his tongue.

Then, when he was finished kissing her, she would curl up, without saying anything to him, with her head on his stomach, covering his navel with her ear, and she would kiss him down there and satisfy him that way.

He didn't say anything to her, but sometimes he grunted. When he finished, he would push her head away gently, and pull the blankets tight over himself, and turn away from her, shutting off the dim, flickering lamp.

She would lie there until the morning, sleeping only five or six hours, but thinking about the lingering taste in her mouth, and the stickiness in her throat. But she was happy that Older Liu did not seem to object, or to be disappointed with her, and she found consolation in this.

The following night, she went to Younger Liu's bedroom. He was sitting there at his little dresser. The layout of the tiny room was exactly the same. The only thing different was the brother – but even the brother, though he was handsomer, was very similar, with the same coloured features, the same hair, the same eyes.

Jade slipped into the bed, wearing nothing but a nightgown. He did not turn to look at her. But after a few moments he stood up and walked over. He crawled on top of her, pulling her nightgown up and kissing her naked body all over. He kissed her neck, sucked on her ears and lips.

She bit his flesh and the joy, the pleasure of it, brought tears to her eyes. She pushed upward to meet him, raising her body from the bed.

One night, hearing these sounds, Older Liu found himself aroused. He could not sleep, and he wanted to see Jade. He waited until their sounds had quieted. Then he got out of his bed and walked over to his brother's room. He knocked softly on the door.

"Younger brother," he said, "can you send Jade to my room, please, if she has a free moment?"

She had never made love to both brothers in the same night, and it was the first time that she considered the possibility of this. She still had the taste of Younger Liu in her mouth. Hearing Older Liu call for her now, knowing that she would shortly be in another man's bed, gave her a secret thrill. She saw herself doing this new

thing, which she had never done before, and her heart jumped at
the thought. She kissed Younger Liu on the lips.

"Come right back when you are finished," he said, looking at
her. Her eyes flashed. He was already in need of her.

She darted out of the room, her hands trembling. She stood
out in the main room for a moment, alone, in silence. She peeked
into Older Liu's bedroom. He was lying there in his bed, waiting
for her.

She could not imagine doing anything with him tonight – it
was bad enough that she had to keep switching men. But two different men in the very same night, even though they were brothers
. . . or maybe it was worse that they were brothers. She did not
know.

She tried to enter the room without losing control, without
panicking or showing her feelings. But she went straight for him,
for Older Liu, without kissing him on the mouth this time. She
ducked into the blankets and seized him in her hands.

Younger Liu was in his bedroom. He had been waiting for
her to finish and come back. But hearing her noises, he found
himself short of breath, frustrated – impatient. He got out of bed,
still undressed, then walked slowly to his door. In the main hall,
he stood at the door of his brother's room. There was a crack. He
could see his brother lying in the bed, with Jade on top of him, her
smooth, white back arched.

Seeing Jade in this state, Younger Liu forgot all about his
brother. He only cared about Jade. How erotic it was, to see his
wife – for Jade was his wife too – with a man.

So he pushed the door open. They did not notice him. He
climbed onto the bed, putting his hands on her slim sides, on her
slender waist, on the curves of her ass.

The next morning, a little later than usual, they sat down at
breakfast. None of them said a word about what had happened.
Jade sat between the two brothers, chewing on a dumpling. They
talked as if everything was normal. They did not seem embarrassed,
and yet they did not look at each other directly in the eyes. Jade sat

there, rubbing the calf of one of them with her dainty foot. And she petted the other with her hand in his lap, squeezing him, and rubbing him gently, slowly, with her thumb.

12.
The Lover

A VEGETARIAN BUFFET OPENED UP NEARBY, ABOUT A HALF-
hour walk from the school. It immediately became my favourite
restaurant and I went a couple times a week if I could. Every time
I went, I had a fear in the pit of my stomach that it would no
longer be there, that it had folded up. The owner was a soft-spoken,
well-mannered Taiwanese gentleman who rode around the city on
a moped.

The shopfront was lime-green, with floor-to-ceiling windows,
a clean, modern look. The employees wore uniforms with orange
aprons and caps. The food was unusually well made, thoughtfully
laid out and of an enormous variety, all for a price, most importantly, that was very reasonable. I had been to Taiwan a few times
and seen similar eateries. Walking off the street, anyone could have
lunch for twenty-five yuan, twenty-two with a Meituan coupon,
and for members twenty yuan. After 1:00 p.m., one could eat or
get a takeout box for fifteen yuan, half the price of a Starbucks coffee. I often got the takeout boxes – the boxes were so big, I could

eat for the next two days. It wasn't just the best restaurant in the city, it was probably the best restaurant I had ever come across, period, and it was right down the street.

Another restaurant, a trendy bistro, occupied part of the same plaza. I had dinner there on one or two occasions, just for comparison. The bistro had awful, overpriced food. The male customers, dolled up in dress shirts and fancy shoes, dangled lit cigarettes from their mouths. The service was slow and the wait staff were rude. Of course, it was impossible to get a table, and the lineups took forever. The live music wasn't too bad. But that was about it.

I was so thankful for the restaurant I liked that when I spotted the owner one day, I shook his hand and had a photo taken with him. "You saved my life," I said. "I was really starving. I've been everywhere in this country, and there's nothing like this."

He didn't know what to say, but simply shook my hand again and patted me on the back.

"What did you say your name was?" he asked. "Dan-ny?"

He thanked me profusely again for visiting his restaurant. Having finished lunch, I went out to the street. I didn't want to go back to the school just yet, so I went over to the shade of a bus shelter. It was the middle of summer, in the midst of sweltering heat, but there was a breeze.

While inspecting the bus routes to see if I could catch a ride back, I saw a young woman walking in my direction. She was wearing nothing more than a rumpled, oversized shirt and red high heels, her naked, toned legs showing like she had forgotten her pants. As she walked by me, her shoe snagged on something, she tripped and the container she was holding spilled onto the pavement.

"Shoot," she said, "there goes my lunch."

"Are you okay?"

"Yeah. But my lunch isn't."

"You can grab something from the buffet over there. The food is pretty good."

She glanced over to the shop I had indicated. Her hopeful face turned dark. "I like meat," she said. "I'm from Dongbei, the North. See how tall I am? That's the secret, lots of meat."

"Oh, okay." As she began to step away, I blurted out, "Say, do you know which bus goes to Yuege Road from here?"

As it turned out, no bus did. She walked with me across the intersection instead. We stopped in front of the China Bank where a red banner promising special deals for new customers snaked in the breeze. I had the sun at my back and she kept having to hold one hand up to keep the light out of her eyes. Her face was beautiful but sweaty and unwashed.

"Hey," I said, "tell me, do you live around here?"

"Not far, why?"

"Nothing really. You look kind of interesting. I thought we could be friends."

"What's the point of friendship?"

"I don't know." I paused, not knowing what else to say. "Where are you going now?"

"I was going home. But I'll have to pick up something else on the way, maybe some octopus balls."

"I'm going back to work. I'm a teacher at the school."

"I don't have a job really. Well, sometimes I work in the KTVs."

I don't know what it was about her, but I wanted to talk to her again. I had never been to the KTVs, and I had never met someone who worked in one.

"So, what do you think, can I have your WeChat?"

She shrugged and took out her phone, squinting in the sunlight.

When I got back to the office, I sent her a message. "Let's meet tomorrow night," I wrote.

"Why do you want to meet me?"

"Because I like you, I want to get to know you better."

I waited a few hours but I didn't hear back from her. Eventually, I gave up and turned my phone off. I had the air conditioner on, but the cramped office felt like it was closing in on me. I opened the tiny window beside my desk and a warm breeze drifted in.

When I looked out, I could see the windows of the neighbouring hotel that occupied the side of the adjacent building. In one of the rooms I could see a young couple, half-naked, sitting on a messy bed, touching but not talking. I closed my window shade. I no longer cared about the fresh air.

The angriest foreign teacher at my school was a six-foot-four American named Clayton. Clayton had never frightened me because he directed all his frustrations toward the school owner and administration, and back then I was nothing more than a teacher like himself. I had often consoled him and even found his outbursts somewhat entertaining.

"You're a smart guy." I put my hand on his shoulder. "You've been here too long." He had become attached to the students and the school, and had strong opinions about how to make it better. But to be honest, I couldn't separate how much of his attitude was true consideration for the students, and how much of it was his ego. He often bullied the support staff, telling them they weren't doing their jobs well, without knowing what their responsibilities were. He constantly harassed the marketing department, especially a lowly, harried female employee whose job it was to recruit new students and clients.

"What do you do?" he shouted in the hallway as the woman walked by. "Why are you paid more than the teachers?"

"I'm 'CC,'" the woman ventured. "Course Consultant."

"You're useless! Why do you get your own office? All you do is call people on the phone. Anybody could do your job. It's the teachers that are important. We're the ones doing all the work."

"I have meetings. I have to find customers."

"The teachers should get more respect and more pay."

"You make more than anyone."

"You make more than the Chinese teachers!" He shook his fist in front of her nose, making her flinch.

"I'm not the one who decides the salaries." The woman began to sob as Clayton marched down the hall and slammed the door behind him.

After work hours, he complained in online discussions that the salaries of the support staff should be halved, though he was clueless what their salaries were. But since the students all loved and encouraged him, his behaviour and attitude became a kind of upward vicious cycle.

He didn't have much education, as many of the foreign teachers didn't. He had never known his father, and wasn't on speaking terms with his mother, who was back in the States. When I first arrived at the school, his passion impressed me, especially for someone who had lost so much. He walked back and forth in the teachers' office, pumping his fist, talking about how this or that needed to be changed so that the students would have a better education.

"I don't know why you care so much," I said. "This place is a dump, and there's hundreds of these schools. In fact, this school is much better than the last one I was at." By the time I had met Clayton, I had worked in over a dozen different schools, so I knew what I was talking about. But there was no point in telling him about myself, and he wasn't interested.

"I've been here for six years," he shouted. "It's been like this the whole time, not one thing has changed."

In his more sensitive moments, he would open up about how lonely he was. By local standards, he was extremely well off working as an American. But he had as yet had no luck with women. I told him that his emotional outbursts scared off potential partners. "You need to control it," I said. "I was like that before, trust me. Meditate, do some yoga or mindfulness." But the loneliness and isolation in his love life only made him even more upset. He was convinced that Chinese people were scared of him, repelled by his skin colour, and I couldn't tell him that wasn't true, because I knew that it was.

"It's racism, they're not attracted to Black men," he said. "The women always say no, but they don't say why. Meanwhile, look at the white guys, mopping up. I deserve love too, don't I? I want to be understood," he half-whispered.

"Didn't you have a girlfriend here before?"

"Her family, her friends, everyone was talking about us. 'Why do you want to be with a Black man? You're not afraid he has AIDS or smuggles drugs? Don't you watch the news on TV?' I loved her, but in the end it wasn't enough."

I nodded, not knowing how to help him. He had his head askew, hung down. His posture, normally defiant and proud, was the opposite: his back curved, his shoulders sagged, he seemed about to topple over. I took a step forward, intending to pat him on the back. But, at the last moment, I thought that a touch from me – a Chinese Canadian man who could pass through this country without any trouble at all – was not what he wanted. Instead, I waved and went out the door.

That week I messaged the young, short-haired woman from Dongbei. This time she seemed to be in a better mood.

"Hey, do you remember me?"

"Yes," she said. "What's up?"

"Have you had lunch? Let me take you out for something to eat."

"Well, I am hungry. There's a really good restaurant, it's Dongbei food. You know pengcai, right?" It was a certain dish made in a big pot with hunks of meat, salty and heavily flavoured, served with a ladle. Just the thought of it made me feel unwell.

"Let me take you to the vegetarian buffet, I really think you'll like it."

"But I told you I hate vegetarian food."

"What do you have to lose? I'm paying for it."

"Okay. I'll meet you there."

She was waiting for me already, in a sheer black dress, the kind of cheap dress with loose threads hanging from the seams that people often bought from Taobao.

"Why are there so many people in this restaurant?" she wondered. "There's not even any meat."

"Maybe because it's cheap, tastes good and it's good for the planet." She made no reply, except to purse her lips and slouch.

We found a small table against the wall. She got a tray and helped herself to some food, although every dish she saw made her scowl in disappointment.

"So," I said, "tell me a bit about yourself, how long have you been in the city?"

"A few years."

She didn't ask me about myself. In fact, she seemed quite bored. She picked at the food on her plate. "This is the last time I'm coming here," she said. "How can you eat this crap?"

She sat back in her chair looking around, exhaling loudly, as if she couldn't wait to leave. "They have no meat, at least they should put some chicken out."

"That would defeat the whole purpose of this restaurant."

"What's the point of coming here? What's the point of eating if there's no meat?"

"Why don't you try some of the soup? It's quite good."

She stood and went over to two metal vats of soup. One was sweet and sour, the other was tofu and egg drop. She shook her head, coming back empty-handed, groaning.

After complaining some more, she ate a few bites. She looked so miserable, I took pity on her. "If you want, we can go somewhere else."

"Forget it," she said. "I've lost my appetite."

Sometime later, Clayton got in a fistfight with the principal. I myself had arrived that day to prepare for a class, only to find the principal's office destroyed – the desks flipped, the computer smashed, a window broken.

"What happened here?" I asked Janey, the acne-scarred financial officer. There had been so many physical altercations, so many violent confrontations, that she was not even in shock.

"Clayton," she said, as if that was all the explanation needed. The police had come on other occasions, but this was the first time that they had taken him to jail and locked him in a cell.

At work the next morning, I was surprised to see Clayton in the classroom teaching. I had assumed that he would be deported or some such thing. But he made so much money for the school that no matter what happened, the owner refused to fire him.

Something else had changed, I noticed. I found all the office furniture rearranged. All the tables, computers and chairs had been cleared out of the two teachers' offices on the third floor and moved into a big classroom on the floor above.

"It was Clayton," said Janey. "He thinks it's better with all the teachers in one room. That way they can communicate more."

The principal's office was still messy. Janey, now the person in charge, was on her knees, cleaning up. Strands of her hair were stuck to her face, sweaty with effort. I didn't bother asking her why Clayton wasn't helping.

The owner, Harold, called the next week and invited me to his headquarters in Shanghai, a massive education centre on top of an office tower, complete with a private movie theatre and roof-top swimming pool. He enjoyed showing off the facilities. I didn't quite understand what it was all for.

"Who uses the swimming pool? The teachers?" I asked.

"Anyone really," he said. "But mostly it's for the students. See, they study hard. Then, everyone knows, they want to take a break. I came up with the idea and had it built last year. There's lots of English centres, but how many have a swimming pool?"

He showed me the sleek classrooms, furnished with state-of-the-art equipment. In the movie theatre, a large empty auditorium with comfortable seating for sixty, he played a promotional video, featuring the history of his company. He was the founder and had won many accolades. At some point in his career, he was given a professorship at a local university, where he taught business.

We made our way down an odd, postmodern hallway, which zigzagged and doubled back on itself, and became narrower and narrower, until we reached a small door, leading to his office. He sat down behind a big desk, and I sat opposite him. He began pouring some hot water and preparing teacups. I had an inkling of what he wanted.

"Did you like that?" he asked.

"Like what?" He nodded toward the door. "The hallway?" It was the weirdest hallway I had ever seen. I felt trapped in the office with him. He gave me a curious smirk. "Did you design it?" I asked.

"Yes" – he grinned – "I designed the whole floor."

"Amazing. You're an artist, a businessman and a professor. Who knows what else?"

"I'm glad you're enjoying this."

"How's the principal?" I asked. "Is he out of the hospital?"

"He's okay. He's still recovering. But he quit."

"He quit?" It was the first time that I had heard the news. I had guessed something like that might have happened. "But did you ask him to stay?"

"He won't stay. He wants Clayton fired, but that's not going to happen, so he quit."

"I see."

"So many problems." Harold threw his head back, rubbing his palms on his face, and groaned. "Clayton's temper is terrible! If only he could control himself."

"Has he always been like this?"

"Let's not talk about the past! The thing is, he's an asset to my company. I'm always a businessman." He handed me a teacup on a saucer. "Danny, let me get to the point. Do you want to be the next principal?"

"Me? Are you sure I'm the right person?"

"My gut tells me so. You have the skills to communicate, you're mature enough. Do you not want to be principal?"

"Yes, but I don't want to be a target for Clayton."

"I have confidence that you'll be able to solve all the problems. I've looked after my company for a long time, I know how to pick my managers. What's more, I'll talk to Clayton, smooth things over. Why don't you take a break, have lunch? After, you can talk to HR and go over the contract."

I took a sip of tea and thought a moment. "You make some good points. But first let me ask, how much does it pay?"

On the train ride back to Hangzhou, I was upbeat. I thought Clayton would be happy that I was principal now. I was a foreign teacher like him. For once, the foreign teachers were in charge of the school. *I'll be able to make all the changes he wants*, I thought.

Four or five of us, the foreign teaching staff, had dinner regularly on weekends. That Saturday was Emma's birthday. In my new role as principal, I bought a birthday cake and brought it to the restaurant.

Steve and Emma were there. "Where's Clayton?" I asked.

"He's angry that you're principal, Danny," Steve said. "I'd watch myself around him. He was hoping that Harold would pick him for the job."

"Clayton as principal?" The idea had never occurred to me.

"Clayton's crazy," Emma said.

"Anyway," Steve continued, "now that you're the boss, what we need is a VPN. The internet is so slow."

"Can we get a feedback box?" Emma asked.

"And make sure we get paid on time," Steve added. "If you don't want Clayton to blow his top."

At school, I occupied my desk in the principal's office, across from Janey. I found a corkboard and erected it between us, sliding it between our desks.

"This way you can't see what I'm up to."

"Sure," she said. "I like it this way too."

I had a bathroom behind me. But it was used for storage, with piles of folders and unused marketing materials, like shirts and hats and bags with the school emblem on them.

I organized meetings, met with concerned parents, looked over new hires. When the regional manager, a guy who blew a lot of hot air, came from Suzhou, I sat opposite him at a long table, with the staff around us, listening to him toot about how we could make our business more effective.

Competing schools had opened up on our street. Next door to us, a restaurant had failed, and a private tutoring centre had moved in, with bright lights and a high-def TV facing the street. Their young employees all looked like handsome and beautiful celebrities, with perfect posture. They even had a foosball table on display. Farther down the street were a dozen other English centres. However, we had been there the longest, and we were the only place licensed to hire foreign staff, so we had a significant advantage.

There was so much to do on that first day. But putting it all aside, I went to work researching VPNs. We didn't have a budget for it, but I knew we could get something, maybe with ads. "Is there any way we can get a feedback box?" I asked Janey.

"You mean something like this?" She showed me some items on Taobao. "I'll order this one. It only costs sixteen yuan." It was a steel box, with a little key, with customizable lettering on its face.

"Where do you think we should put it up?"

"On the stairwell landing, out of sight of the cameras," I said. "People won't want to give us feedback if they're on camera."

A couple weeks passed without too much excitement. Mostly the job entailed making sure the foreign staff came to work on time. If one of them couldn't make it to class, I would have to put every-thing aside and act as the substitute teacher. I figured that was what Harold had in mind when he'd hired me for the job.

Lately, Clayton had been deliberately missing his classes. "Are you going to show up today?" one of the secretaries asked him over the phone.

"Yes," he shouted, before hanging up. As it turned out, the students sat in the classroom without a teacher, waiting and waiting. Sometimes he showed up after fifteen minutes, only to give a ten-minute rant about how terrible the school was, before taking off again without a word.

There were plenty of ways for him to undermine the daily routine. A few weeks before, he had been booted from the school's WeChat group, which included hundreds of students, parents, teachers and support staff, for clogging up the message board with dozens of lines of explicit language and threats of righteous violence. Now he had formed his own WeChat group, made up of a few confused but loyal students, as well as three disgruntled employees who had been terminated in the preceding months.

Maybe he figured, after punching the previous principal, he would never be fired. When the end of the month came, I knew Harold planned to retaliate by withholding Clayton's pay.

"Janey, do we have enough money for Clayton's salary?" I asked.

She shook her head. "All the revenue goes straight to Harold's bank account, in Shanghai."

I called Harold. "Please, can you transfer the money for salaries now?"

"I'll get to it soon," Harold said. "You have my word, it won't be late."

That weekend, however, I found a bunch of texts and missed calls on my phone. I hurried over to school to find a police cruiser there.

I could hear Clayton shouting from above. "Where's my money?" he was yelling. "Late again, late again!" I rushed up to the fourth floor and found a pair of sheepish police officers standing near the stairwell. The yelling was coming from down the hallway, behind some closed doors.

"What's going on?" I asked. The officers shrugged. I ran over to the office door and found it locked. I could hear Clayton yelling and Janey sobbing.

"Hey, Clayton, open the door," I said, somewhat feebly. Before I could knock a second time, it swung open. He towered over me. Behind him was Janey, normally chirpy. She was huddled in a corner, acne flushed red, her frizzy black hair covering her tear-streaked face.

"I've been locked in here for an hour," she choked, as she wobbled up from where she had been crouched on the floor and hurried by me.

Clayton continued with his fist-pounding routine. He pushed me against the door and followed Janey out into the hallway.

"Where do you think you're going?" Clayton shouted at the financial officer. He pushed and herded her into another room.

"Clayton!" I waved to get his attention.

He smashed his hands together an inch from my face. "So you showed up. Think I don't know what you did?" He yelled so loud my knees buckled. He held his fist up to my nose, then cocked back, like he was about to clobber me between the eyes. At the last moment, he let his hand fall, and then laughed in my face.

"I should be principal," he shouted, striding up and down the hallway. "You stole that job from me. I've been here for six years! I've got good ideas. I'm the one who got rid of what's-his-face," referring to the principal he had punched. "When I was in jail, did you come see me? Did any of you?"

He went on, letting loose a tirade that made me cower. "I've done so much for this school but in the end they picked you over me. Why? Tell me, what's the reason?" He grabbed me by the collar with both hands and shook me, shouting in my face. I hadn't time to react when he shouted, "Is it because I'm Black? You know why, you all know why."

He went out to the balcony, overlooking the quiet, tree-lined street, bellowing to passersby, children, cars and cyclists. "I don't want anything now except my money. Give me my money! Money, give me money!" The police were there, but they stood off to the side, tiptoeing back and forth, keeping their distance.

Finally, after half an hour more, he left on his own, slamming the front door so hard the wooden frame cracked from top to bottom.

This was all normal business for the school, apparently, as the owner seemed unconcerned.

"This is getting a bit out of hand, don't you think?" I said, over the phone. "Maybe you should talk to him yourself, come to some sort of understanding."

"Not to worry. I spoke to the police. They said they'll keep an eye on him."

I didn't feel reassured at all.

The men's washroom was across the hall from my office. I tried to avoid it whenever I could because of the inevitable stench of urine and, perhaps worse, the cigarette smoke. I always held my breath until I was done my business. As I was finishing up at the urinal, my phone beeped in my pocket.

The stale air of the hallway was a relief. Inside my office, I slipped my phone out and found a message.

"Let's do something this evening. You still want to see me, right?"

"Of course."

"Okay, as long as we don't go to that awful cabbage restaurant you like. What do you want to do?"

"Let's go watch a movie."

"There are no good movies out," she replied. "How about taking me to a spa?"

I wasn't sure what she meant by 'spa,' but as it turned out, she meant a footbath. We met at a place called Lotong Wooden Foot Palace, a popular family chain that served couples and families.

I had passed by this place before, though I had never been inside. It was sumptuously decorated: the front desk was trimmed in wood and gold paint, with a fountain trickling water down the wall behind it, and four professional female clerks at the ready, along with two young men in vests holding their hands behind their backs.

"It's sixty for a foot massage, plus thirty for a toenail trimming," she said. "That's one hundred and twenty for the both of us, plus the thirty for me."

"I think I'll just watch, if that's okay."

"Oh? How come? You can get a girl to massage you, it won't be a guy, you know."

"I know. I just don't like people touching my feet."

She shrugged and took a step away from the counter to give me room to pay. I didn't mind paying for her. It made sense now why she had changed her mind about seeing me. She was treating herself to a free massage at my expense. "You sure you don't want a massage too?" she asked, as I paid the bill. "It feels really good, it's my favourite way of relaxing."

The whole place was designed in a traditional style, like a tea house. Passing by a low-lying table, I picked some complimentary treats out of a bowl. They had packets of spiced dried green peas and other snacks. "Don't worry," she said. "There's free food, as much as you want, it comes included."

We picked a small room on the first floor and sat in the lush sofa chairs. An enormous flat-screen TV was built into the wall, but it just so happened that the sound system was broken.

"We don't need to turn it on anyway. Are you sure you don't want to have a foot massage too?"

I shook my head. "I'll just sit here and relax."

She pressed a button by the side of the door. In a moment an attendant came to take our orders. "We'll have two tea eggs to start, and a white flower soup and some fruit. And tea of course."

"Jasmine or green tea?"

"Green."

She wore a cheap red Taobao dress with spaghetti straps with see-through mesh covering her chest and upper arms. That style had spread virally online through Douyin and I had seen that dress everywhere, on women of all ages.

I tried sitting closer to her, which wasn't a simple task. The chairs were large. Separating us was a small table with tissues and an ashtray. I managed to prop myself up onto the arm of my chair, and lean across. I didn't get much information out of her, except to ask about the KTV where she worked, a question she regarded without interest. Our conversation was cut short when the server returned with our food. A second attendant, a good-looking, lean, young man, entered and began setting up a wooden tub filled with hot water at her feet.

I got comfortable in the oversized, cushy chair. Only one attendant stayed, massaging first her back, shoulders, head, then calves. I kept quiet most of the time. The two of them spoke, my date and her handsome young attendant.

After a few sips of her tea and soup, she looked at me. "Do you mind if I order some spicy octopus balls?" She took out her phone and swiped over to her Meituan app. "I love the barbequed octopus balls from this shop, they're the best in the city."

She had her bare feet soaking in the tub while the attendant massaged her shoulders. I didn't have much to do except play on my phone and listen to them. I learned more about her from the way she carried on a conversation. She wasn't a timid girl at all.

When she was finished soaking, the attendant dried and began massaging her feet, her legs naked to the hem of her dress. Her phone rang. "We're on the first floor, come over here, just ask the front desk," she said into her phone. The way she spoke was always a yell. We could hear the loud voices out in the hall, and the echoes. A moment later there was a knock on the door, which had been ajar.

"Oh, it's you," the delivery boy said. "I thought it was, but the address was different, so I wasn't sure."

"I usually order from home, but today I'm here. You were fast!" She laughed her chuckling, boyish laugh. "You're so far away, I wasn't sure you'd deliver." They were waiting for me to pay, so I took out my little satchel.

I looked in the paper bag. It wasn't just octopus balls, it was chicken wings and some sauces and napkins. She offered me some, but I wasn't hungry in the least.

"Too bad we can't order pengcai. Imagine if they came here with a huge wok and started cooking right in front of us?" She turned to her attendant. "You're doing a good job, it's just the right strength," she said. "How many people have you done today? You must be tired." It was easy enough for me to sit there and be her company without doing anything. In a way, I was glad that the attendant was there to do the talking.

"I need this. Look at the heels I wear."

Before I knew it, the attendant had left. We were alone in the room, it was late already, and she was getting ready to go.

"Wait," I said, "let's spend some more time together."

"Why? I'm tired, I want to go home."

The whole evening we hadn't said much to each other. The foot attendant had made her laugh more than I had. Maybe it was primal male desperation or competitive spirit that gave me the courage, but I sat down on the arm of her chair.

"How about if we kiss?" I asked.

"Why? No." She made a face and tried to get up. "Aren't you a vegetarian? I just ate octopus balls."

I laughed. "I don't care about that."

I leaned forward and waited. She let out a somewhat exasperated sigh and finally kissed me. Once our lips touched, I could feel her body relax and all her resistance give way. I didn't care what else happened that night. Somehow I knew I would see her again, that she was the one for me. My loneliness, that feeling Clayton must have known for so long, had evaporated. When I stood upright, she was holding onto my hand and looking up into my eyes.

"Are you busy now?" she asked.

"No, why?"

"Let's go get a hotel room."

Her voice was so earnest there was no mistaking her meaning. When I studied her face for clues, I saw that she was breathless and wild-eyed. It wasn't something a woman had said to me before. Call me old-fashioned, but I had never slept with a woman on a first date – or even a second date. I was a little scared.

"It was just a kiss," I said. "We don't know each other really well. Let's go on another date tomorrow instead."

To my surprise, she insisted. "I haven't slept with anyone for a long time." I thought she was joking, but she stared at me, her face dead serious, her lips trembling.

After a quick car ride, we found a fancy hotel. She sat in the lobby, fidgeting on the sofa, while I went to the concierge and paid for a room. Upstairs, in front of the curtained window, she stripped off her clothes. I watched, mesmerized.

"Well? Don't you have a condom?"

I shook my head. It had never occurred to me that I would need one. "Should I go out and buy some?"

"Look over there." She pointed to the bathroom. "Hurry up." Inside, by the sink, was a straw basket lined with soap, combs, toothbrushes and the like. Among these items, I found a shiny wrapped box of three condoms.

Lying together in bed, we embraced.

"I'm . . . not used to this," I said.

"What? Sleeping with a woman?"

"No, I mean, moving so fast."

"I didn't have any feelings," she said. "But when we kissed, I did. Now, come on, what are you doing?" For some reason, I felt a bit off, intimidated maybe because she was so attractive, so casual and comfortable with herself.

Somehow, a key moment passed, and I knew it. She was waiting for me, but I didn't respond. I wasn't used to that kind of pressure. The room had two queen-sized beds, and, sensing her hostility, I lay down by myself on the spare one.

She was stretched out, looking over. "I can't believe this," she said, flinging her words. "If you don't get to it, I'm leaving." I went back and lamely tried to kiss her, but she kicked me away.

"Put on a condom."

When I failed, she got up, laughing in my face, and threw on her clothes.

"Don't ever call me again," she shouted as she disappeared out the door.

I stayed in the room for another few hours, watching a movie on the wide-screen TV, picking through the snacks in a bowl on the desk. It was past midnight when I left, when I stood in the brightly lit lobby, watching the quiet street and the doorman, pacing.

The next day I got up late. On the way to work, filled with pity for myself, I thought about her and about what had happened. I arrived to find the school quiet as usual, but a peculiar sensation came over me. I walked up and down the halls, looking through the glass walls at the students and teachers busying themselves. I poked my head into the teachers' room; nobody was there.

In my office I found Janey. "Is Clayton around?" I asked.

"Didn't you hear? He got a job at a different school. He already cleared out his desk."

Just like that, he was out of my life. I sat down in my swivel chair and leaned back, thinking about the news. In my pocket was a letter I had written to him in the night. I took it out and unfolded it, wondering if I should find a way to send it to him. I had taken the job that was his, and I had squandered the love that he couldn't have. I wanted to tell him that he was right about the school, about the kind of person I was, about the unfairness of the country and its people. I wished that he would find peace with himself and the world, such as it was.

Instead, I tore the letter in two and threw it in the garbage. Then I went back to work.

Acknowledgements

I BEGAN THIS COLLECTION IN MY FIRST YEAR IN CHINA AS a student at Capital Normal University in Beijing. I want to thank the people I knew then, in particular: Fan Yu Ping, Chang Yu and Huang Jin Lin. There were others, including my uncle, Allan Chung in Hong Kong, who gave me much support. And then there was Joan Zhou – Zhou Hu Qiong – whom I wish I could see again.

Many thanks to my editor, Jen Sookfong Lee. If I could have just one reader in the world, I would choose Jen. I also want to thank the team at Wolsak & Wynn, especially Noelle Allen, Paul Vermeersch, Jennifer Hale, Michel Vrana, Tania Blokhuis and Ashley Hisson, for all their hard work and expertise.

I am also grateful to friends, mentors and fellow writers: Fatima Abbas, Erika Loic, Gaston Cox, Ron Schafrick, Peter Woolstencroft, Tim Brook and Sarah Koetsier. Thanks to Greg Maloney who read some of the earliest drafts.

Finally, I would like to thank my parents, Connie and Milton Woo, and my brothers and their families: James, Humie, Ella, Marissa, Ken, Sarah, Alex and Henry. Most of all, thanks to Wan, the best singing partner and wife I could ask for.

DAN K. WOO travelled and worked in Hong Kong and Mainland China for over a decade. In 2018 he won the Ken Klonsky Award for *Learning How to Love China* (Quattro Books). His writing has appeared in such publications as the *South China Morning Post, Quill & Quire* and *China Daily USA*. Dan taught English at Fanshawe College in London, Ontario, and now occasionally teaches creative writing at the University of Toronto School of Continuing Studies. A Toronto native, he lives with his partner in the city and works for cybersecurity start-up GoSecure.